Second Chance Ranch

A Hope Springs Novel

Sometimes love is right where you left it.

Sadie Hart has a plan: return to her small town of Hope Springs so she can regain her confidence—and bank account—before giving one more shot to her country music dream. The dream that means more to her than anything. The dream she chose over her high school sweetheart, the brooding and sinfully handsome Royce Dixon.

Royce has moved on from his memories of the beautiful Sadie. Now he's focused solely on running Second Chance Ranch, where he rehabilitates troubled teens through ranch work. But when he needs a new employee and Sadie's the only one to volunteer, he has no choice but to offer his old flame a job.

Whether riding a horse with the wind in her hair or mucking out the stalls, Sadie can still get Royce's heart beating like no one else. But Nashville is her dream, and Royce can't settle for second best.

SECOND CHANCE RANCH

A HOPE SPRINGS NOVEL

CINDI MADSEN

Entangled Publishing, LLC
2614 South Timberline Road
Suite 109
Fort Collins, CO 80525
Visit our website at www.entangledpublishing.com.

Bliss is an imprint of Entangled Publishing, LLC. For more information on our titles, visit http://www.entangledpublishing.com/category/bliss

Edited by Stacy Abrams
Cover design by Jessica Cantor

Ebook ISBN 978-1-63375-070-8
Print ISBN 978-1-50231-781-0

Manufactured in the United States of America

First Edition September 2014

To my grandpa Gaylon, for being one of the best guys I know and for stopping by my car anytime he saw it around town to check the oil. And to my grandma Doris, who cured all ills with food and talks at the kitchen table—I miss and cherish those talks.
To both of you, for always being there and for being a great example of what love is.

Chapter One

Time travel had always been on Sadie's list of impossible things that could never happen, but here she was, warped back six years, everything the exact same except for her. Time travel was both easier and harder than she'd imagined. It involved a flight from Nashville, Tennessee, to Gillette, Wyoming—during the last leg of which she'd prayed for her soul with every bump the tiny plane hit—and an hour drive in a truck several years older than she was. Hope Springs, Wyoming, looked exactly the same, practically untouched by time. Same houses. Same stores. Same oh-my-gosh-I'm-in-the-middle-of-nowhere feeling. The rest of the world could implode, and here in the Town That Time Forgot, people would simply go about their daily lives.

Grandpa slowed as they came to Main Street, resting his wrist on top of the steering wheel in that casual manner with which the entire town ran. As the truck idled in front of the Dairy Freeze that held a thousand memories in and of itself,

Sadie remembered a warm night in August when she was nineteen and riding in a truck about this old, with a guy not nearly as old as her current riding companion.

A handsome face flashed through her mind—eyes lit up, a smile curving the lips she had memorized, both by sight and feel. Just the memory was enough to tug on her heartstrings, waking them up from years of enforced dormancy. That night all those years ago, she'd turned down one dream for another, and she'd wondered at least a hundred times since if she'd chosen wrong.

All she'd ever wanted to be was a country music star. But the music industry had chewed her up and spit her out, and the only thing she had to show for her last six years of hard work was a bank account so low on funds that buying a pack of gum might send her into the red.

So here she was, in the place she'd avoided as much as possible since high school, a heavy side of defeat pressing down on her.

"They redid the theater," Grandpa said, gesturing to the building with multicolored flashing lights. Apparently, one thing *had* actually changed. "It's got six screens now, can you imagine? Who's got time to go to that many movies? And the tickets are up to eight fifty." He shook his head. "I tell you. Don't know what this world's coming to."

Sadie smiled at Grandpa, a surge of affection for him rising up. She doubted he'd even been to a movie in the new building. He always said that he didn't see the sense in going to the theater when you could just wait a few months and watch it a lot cheaper, without having to sit next to a bunch of strangers. Which always struck her as funny since, in this tiny town, you'd be hard-pressed to find a stranger.

Part of her was glad things hadn't drastically changed, and the other part felt the cold stab of truth piercing her chest. She'd failed. And all of these people she'd thought she was going to pass by—as in she'd have a real life while they stayed here and never lived up to their potential—had passed *her* by. Mom's phone calls were filled with news of marriages and babies and promotions at places like one of the two banks or the few hotels. Or, for instance, when the Smiths got the highest price in the county for their corn *and* their cows.

This is just a minor setback, though. Okay, so maybe more like a major *setback, but still, totally temporary. I'll brush myself off, take a little time to recover, and bounce right back, stronger than ever.*

The springs in the seat of Grandpa's truck squeaked and rocked as he pulled into the shopping center. "I've gotta go drop off your grandma's prescription. While I wait for the medicine, maybe you can take care of this shopping list for your mom?"

He gave her a handwritten list along with a hundred-dollar bill. She glanced from the pharmacy to Homeland Foods, a couple of shops separating them. Of course there wasn't a pharmacy *in* the grocery store. And even if there were, her grandparents never trusted places that multitasked, as if the pharmacist in a grocery store might mix up and give you pills with lettuce in them by accident.

The odds of seeing someone she knew were around 99.5 percent. She was sure the town's entire population had heard about her performance at Tyler Blue's induction to the Louisiana Music Hall of Fame, and everyone she ran into would want to know why they hadn't heard her singing on the radio yet—something she'd assumed would happen shortly after that performance in Louisiana, too.

That was before everything had fallen apart, though, and after the last time she'd gotten on a stage…well, she didn't want to think about it, because she was fighting bursting into tears as it was.

There'd also be questions about how long she'd be in town, and since she looked like crap from traveling on top of all that cheeriness, Homeland Foods was the last place she wanted to go. But it's not like she could say, *No, Grandpa, I need to primp and mentally prepare before buying food that's, you know, necessary for life.*

So she just smiled. "No problem."

Luckily there weren't many items on the list. She strode into the market, grabbed a basket, and shopped as if she were in a high-stakes race. At the last minute, she paused in front of the condiments. Green olives weren't on Grandpa's list, but he and Sadie used to sneak into the kitchen late at night and down a jar between them, along with large glasses of chocolate milk. He even used to joke that all the olives she'd eaten were how her eyes got to be so green. Just in case, she grabbed a jar and headed to the next aisle over to pick up a canister of Nesquik. She took one last glance at the list.

Looks like I got it all. Miracle of miracles, she'd managed to avoid running into anyone she knew. All she had to do was get out of here and back to the safety of Grandpa's truck.

But then she turned, and the world ground to a screeching halt. The guy she'd just been thinking about—the one who'd offered her another dream all those years ago—was coming down the aisle. She darted out of sight, her heart jumping around like crazy. A thump and a squeeze, and she was starting to get light-headed with how fast it was going.

What was Royce Dixon, her high school boyfriend and the guy who'd asked her to marry him all those years ago, doing in Homeland Foods right now?

And how the hell could she get out of here without him seeing her?

. . .

Royce grabbed the jumbo jar of peanut butter, picked up raspberry and grape jam—they always seemed to be the favorites—and made his way to the checkout stands. As usual, his mind was still back at the ranch, spinning over everything he needed to get done and how behind he was. Being shorthanded was starting to become a huge problem. Important things were falling by the wayside, and with the new batch of teens for the camp just in, he desperately needed another employee, and he needed one now. Especially after the bomb his lawyer had decided to drop today. Everyone in town was busy working their own jobs, and most of them had ranch work, too. He'd asked around—even taken out an ad—and had gotten squat. Not even one person.

And now it didn't just need to be a person. It needed to be a *she*.

Royce pressed his fingers to the throbbing headache forming between his temples. Working with troubled teens brought all sorts of extra issues and liabilities, and apparently he was putting himself at risk every single day that there wasn't another female adult around. Mom couldn't be everywhere at once, not to mention she couldn't be confined to the ranch full-time.

The appointment with Mr. Blackstone was supposed to be simple, just a few signatures and papers being notarized, all the t's crossed and i's dotted, the way they always had to be when a new batch of teens came in. *I can't believe I thought I was at least almost on top of the alternative youth camp side of things.*

The lawyer had told him there was a case going on the next county over where a woman had filed a sexual harassment complaint against the owners of a dude ranch. The guy she'd accused claimed she was just mad because he'd rebuffed her advances, but the all-male staff made it look worse, and now the owner might lose his ranch, regardless of what had really happened.

"He put himself in a bad situation," Mr. Blackstone had said. "And you are, too. It's a liability you can't afford, Royce, especially not with a bunch of bitter teenagers around. You've got to cover your assets."

Royce had wanted to tell him that he'd just forget about the youth camp side of the ranch, then. He could focus on the horses he had and take on more work training roping horses, which was what he was better at anyway. Horses came naturally—teens, not so much.

But then he'd thought of Mom's face. How it'd drop, and there'd no doubt be tears involved. The Alternative Ranch Camp for Youth was her dream, one that Dad had bent over backward to make happen and had spent countless hours helping her run. Royce knew he made a poor substitute. After Dad passed away, Mom had thrown herself even more into the youth camp. She was always coming up with new ideas. Pushing them to do more, with less time in between.

It was how she'd dealt with the grief, and Royce knew it was what kept her getting up every day, no matter how much she missed her husband.

So he'd asked Mr. Blackstone what he needed to do, and the lawyer suggested he hire another woman to work at the camp—or even the ranch, as long as she was around to help balance out the genders on the adult side. Otherwise Royce was opening himself up for a lawsuit, and if that happened, someone could go after not just the camp but also the entire ranch. A ranch that had been in his family for three generations.

Shit. What the hell am I going to do? Especially since I've already got two cabins of teens at the ranch?

His headache doubled in size, a heavy sense of urgency coming along with it. Royce neared the front of the store, and he wasn't sure exactly why, but the hairs on his arms and the back of his neck rose. Only one checkout stand had a light on, and there was a skinny girl with a messy blond bun putting her groceries on the conveyor belt. There was something about her…

She glanced over her shoulder and then immediately whipped her head forward.

Everything inside of him turned cold and hard, and it felt like he'd been punched in the gut.

It couldn't be…but he knew it was. The glimpse of her profile had been enough. She didn't used to be so thin, and her hair used to be more of a strawberry than a platinum blond, but the way she held her head, the curve of her neck—the way everything inside of him was pulled to her, regardless of all the years that had passed…

Sadie Hart. The girl who'd made him fall in love and then

left him without a second thought. Resentment came then, thankfully clearing out that wussy, weak sensation that'd first clenched his body. For years he'd wondered when he would turn on the radio and hear her familiar voice belting out a love song. He'd dreaded it so badly, but part of him wished for it, too. He would've changed the station, but regardless of all that had happened, he'd like to think there would've been a glimmer of pride over the fact that she'd made it.

Sadie glanced back again and winced, but she didn't look away this time. As much as he didn't want to see her, her wide-eyed, struggling-for-air expression said that right now, he had the upper hand.

So he plastered on a smile and moved closer.

She picked up a jar and held it in her hands like some kind of lifeline, her knuckles white and her face pale. "R-Royce. Hi."

It was so mean, the words on the tip of his tongue, but he said them anyway. "Why, if it isn't the famous Sadie Hart. I'm still waiting to hear you on the radio. When's that gonna happen, by the way?"

Her face paled even more, her eyes blinking rapidly like she might cry, and a twinge of regret went through him. The girl had hardly ever been without a giant smile—not just that, but if anyone had dared to frown around her, she'd use it on him or her and add a joke or two, not letting up until she got a smile back. He'd never been able to see Sadie sad without taking it on himself to fix it, the way she did with everyone else.

But that was all before. *Why didn't I just keep my big mouth shut so we could both pay for our groceries and get out of here as quickly as possible?*

"Well...I..." Sadie twisted the jar in her hands, and it slipped loose and hit the floor with a loud crash. She quickly dropped down, scooping at the shattered remains and gathering up slimy green olives while muttering swear words.

Royce squatted down, guilt at pushing her now forming a lump in his gut. "Stop picking it up. You're going to get glass in your fingers."

"I have eyes," she spat at him. "I can see the glass, and I'll just grab the edges."

He gritted his teeth. "Fine. Slice your fingers off for all I care."

"Thanks for that. And for the singing comment. You're as charming as I remember."

"Right back at you, sweetheart." He stood, irritation tightening his muscles, a layer of frustration under it. Okay, the singing comment had been an ass move, but he'd immediately felt bad, and he sincerely was trying to keep her from hurting herself. How had he managed to forget how quickly her temper flared? Or how it sent a sexy flush of red across her cheeks?

Lucy, the cashier, looked on at the mess and Sadie, chewing her gum and not bothering to call for help or put forth more than minimal effort into her job.

"Ouch!" Sadie brought up her finger and sucked on it.

Royce leaned a hip on the edge of the conveyor belt. "Cut yourself, didn't you?"

She glared up at him and straightened, getting right in his face like she used to whenever they argued. It wasn't like they'd been one of those couples who always fought; they were just one of those couples who didn't always agree and were passionate about it.

"You know what?" she asked, jabbing a finger in his chest. As much as he shouldn't be turned on by it, he sort of was, the blood in his veins pumping faster and hotter than it had in a long time. He waited for her insult, anticipating what he could say back. But then her face suddenly fell and she sighed. "I'm too tired to do this right now. And I don't even know what I'm doing. I'm just getting groceries, and I didn't expect…" Her gaze lifted to his, and he forgot how to breathe for a second. While everything else about her looked slightly different, the dark green eyes were the same. He'd been focused on the glint of anger, but now he could see the softer side. The vulnerable side that used to make him want to curl her into his arms and protect her from the rest of the world.

Damn, now he was getting mushy, and he couldn't let her do that to him. He wasn't the guy she'd left behind for Nashville anymore, full of optimism and thinking all he needed was his horse, his truck, and his girl by his side and life would be perfect.

He gestured toward Lucy. "I think she's waiting for you to pay for your groceries."

Sadie glanced at the cashier, nodded, and then held out the money. "Sorry about the olives. I'll just take the rest of the groceries, and I guess you'll have to call for a cleanup or whatever."

Now he felt bad again. He wasn't sure if Sadie was in town for a visit or if she planned on staying awhile—no doubt he'd hear the gossip soon enough—but he needed to stay away from her. The woman was toxic, and there was no way he'd let her mess with his heart or his head ever again.

. . .

Sadie glanced at Royce as the cashier took the hundred-dollar bill from her.

He looked so much the same. Still tall—although she swore he'd grown another inch or two—chestnut hair shot with golden streaks from hours in the sun, despite the fact he wore a hat most of the time, and deep brown eyes. He'd filled out since high school, too, his chest stretching the fabric of his shirt, his defined arms several inches bigger around than they used to be. Like when she'd been in high school, she got a little breathless when she looked at him. It was one of the reasons she'd almost given up her singing dream and married him, regardless of the fact that they'd barely been out of high school.

Memories flooded her, snippets from nights in the back of his truck, legs tangled together, his hand in her back pocket, the starry sky overhead as the thump of his beating heart sounded against her ear. Even after she'd left, her heart ached for him for months afterward, a piece of it gone that she knew she'd never get back or be able to replace.

Realizing she was staring, she lowered her gaze, idly taking in the groceries he'd placed on the conveyor belt. Supplies to make peanut butter and jelly sandwiches for a year, a giant bag of pancake mix and a jug of syrup, a case of Coke and one of Coors.

"You can buy beer now," she said, finding it almost funny after how much effort they used to go to get it in high school.

"It's one of my proudest accomplishments." There was plenty of sarcasm in his words, but there was a hint of amusement in them, too. Her eyes drifted back to his as if they couldn't help themselves, and his expression immediately morphed into a distant, tight-lipped one. Would it kill him to try to make this run-in easier?

There was so much she wanted to say, but she didn't even know how to start, and considering the way her thoughts and emotions were whirring, she was pretty sure anything that came out would just be gibberish.

The cashier waved a couple of bills in front of Sadie's face. "Um, here's your change."

Sadie took it out of her hands and noticed Grandpa standing next to the exit doors. Thank goodness. She'd needed to get out of here about ten minutes ago. Where was the damn time machine now?

After gathering her bags of food, Sadie headed toward Grandpa. For some stupid reason, she couldn't help glancing back at her ex-boyfriend again, even though common sense told her to run as fast as possible.

He wasn't looking at her, though. He was making small talk with the cashier. Going on with his life.

Probably the exact same way he'd done every day since she'd left this godforsaken town.

As soon as they were settled into the truck, Grandpa glanced at her. "You talk to him?"

He always could read her better than anyone else. There was no point in even asking who, or acting as though running into Royce hadn't affected her. "Not really."

The guy she hadn't really talked to came out of Homeland Foods, and she watched him walk to a beat-up, mostly blue pickup truck. He opened the door and she noticed the white sign with the dark blue words DIXON HORSE RANCH &

ARCFY on the side of it.

"He still running both Dixon Ranch and Second Chance Ranch?" Sadie asked.

Technically, it was named the Alternative Ranch Camp for Youth, but since it was a program for troubled teens, people around here had nicknamed it Second Chance Ranch. Basically there were several studies that proved equine assisted therapy—putting people who had troubles with violence, depression, low self-esteem, et cetera, with horses—helped them. Some of the teens were sent because their parents thought they needed discipline or they didn't know how to get through to them anymore, and some were court ordered to attend and prove they deserved to be back in society instead of picking up trash on the highway or sent to juvie. She'd always admired the Dixons for running it, and on her frequent visits to the ranch, she'd seen how much work it took for his parents to keep it going.

Guilt seeped in, filling her lungs. When she'd heard about Royce's dad passing, her first instinct was to fly home and see if Royce needed her. At that time, though, nearly five years had already passed since they'd spoken, she was playing back-to-back gigs with two other girls she was briefly in a band with, and she didn't know if he'd want her there anyway.

"Doin' a damn fine job of it, too," Grandpa said. "When Jim died, all these people in town were talking, the way they do, implying he wouldn't be able to keep both running. There was lots of speculation he'd close the youth camp in favor of keepin' up the horse ranch. But you should see the place now." Grandpa started up the truck and it rumbled to life. "He and his mom have made it work. She does the counseling side of things, and Royce takes care of most everything else, including training roping horses for people around the state. Cory Brooks works out there with them, too."

Cory Brooks was Royce's best friend going all the way back to preschool, and Sadie was glad they'd found a way to work together, the way they'd always planned on growing up. Even though she was the one who'd moved away, an unexpected pang of being left out hit her. The three of them used to forever be scrunched in the cab of a pickup truck, headed to the next rodeo. If her best friend, Quinn Sakata, had gotten permission from her parents to go with them, they'd take a truck with an extended cab so they could all fit, but those times had been few and far between.

"They've had a few people come and go, and a couple of others work part-time, but those three keep it running somehow," Grandpa continued. "And while there's the occasional person who still raises a fuss about the supposed hoodlums being so close to town, there hasn't been an incident since Royce took over."

"What about the rodeo stuff? Is he still competing?"

"Oh, he usually does a couple of the local ones, but other than that…" Grandpa shook his head. "Don't think he has the time—even before Jim passed on, he was doing less and less to try to keep up with the ranch."

Sadie watched Royce's truck turn down the road that led out of town as Grandpa turned in the other direction. She used to love that ranch, so much so that his place became her second home. More scenes of racing horses to the river, kisses on a blanket laid out next to the rushing water, and nights when kissing turned into more, played out in her mind, seeming more like dreams than real memories. While she might have to drive by just to see what the place looked like now, she'd never have the guts to go ask for the tour. Over the years, she'd tried her hardest to stamp out the longing that she felt whenever she thought of Dixon Ranch and the guy who lived there.

Don't even start with that depressing line of thinking.

What she needed to focus on was getting a job, getting back on her feet, and then figuring out a way to get back to Nashville and her singing career. There were too many ghosts here, and the last thing she needed were more reminders of all the ways she'd failed at life.

Chapter Two

Royce turned up the radio, Aerosmith blasting from the classic rock station as he drove toward the ranch. At first he was trying to drown out thoughts of Sadie Hart, but it wasn't working, so he decided to take them on instead. Objectively, she was still pretty, but it was like she'd spent the past few years getting rid of everything unique about her. The curves were gone, replaced by the too-thin type of body that was so popular in Hollywood—and Nashville, apparently. Her strawberry-blond waves had been lightened so much that none of the reddish hue remained, which was a shame. At least she still had those large green eyes and the adorable freckles scattered across her nose and cheeks that stood out even more when her skin flushed pink.

Her temper's definitely still in place. He found himself smiling at that—they used to verbally spar, all in good fun, their own sort of foreplay. The girl was passionate to the point of being blind to anything but her opinion, and when he dared to have a different one, her voice would rise higher and higher, and then he'd get fired up right back. Eventually he'd just pull her into his arms and kiss her until she sagged against him. It was the one weapon he could use to persuade her to see his side the tiniest bit.

His blood heated thinking about the countless kisses they'd shared. The nights lying out under the stars, cuddled under a thin blanket with nothing else between them, knowing they didn't have long before one of their parents would be calling or texting to ask where they were.

For a moment, he was lost to the memories he'd kept locked away for years, and he wanted to go back and redo their meeting in the grocery store. Tease out a smile and see if it was still the same. Hear her laugh.

Then he remembered that the girl had ripped out his heart. He tightened his grip on the wheel. Sure, he was over it now, but it'd taken longer than he cared to admit. He'd learned his lesson, too. Nice guys *did* finish last. It wasn't like he'd become a jerk, but he'd been more on guard during his short-lived other relationships. The more he blew off or pushed away a woman, the more aggressively she pursued him. It made no logical sense, but the female population ate that up. Until the moment she realized he was simply that busy with the ranch and not interested in putting forth enough effort to make it work on a deeper level.

The ranch. How the hell am I going to find someone who's good with the teens and *the animals?* He'd been struggling to find someone already, and that was before cutting the prospects at least in half by needing to hire a female employee. Which was probably something he couldn't say, either, or he'd just be giving more people cause to sue him.

Right now he'd settle for someone good with one or the other. He, Cory, and Mom could pick up the slack on the other side.

A thick cloud of dust kicked up behind him as he turned onto the dirt road leading home. The cabins, barn, and fence sharpened into relief as he neared, all black outlines against the dark sky. He knew the position he needed filled involved hard work, and the pay was nothing to brag about, but it was all he could afford. The last two people he'd hired had lasted about a year each before quitting. One moved away, and one took a job at the hospital after her relationship with Cory fizzled out—Royce should've known dating coworkers was a disaster waiting to happen. Especially when one of them was Cory, who never could maintain a relationship for shit.

Royce pulled up to his house and cut the engine. The lights were only on in the girls' cabin, so the boys were probably there, too. He sent Mom a quick text to check in, and she replied that she was playing games with the kids. She added that she'd send the boys to their cabin soon.

At least that's taken care of. Of all the things that could fall through, the teens couldn't be one of them. They needed constant supervision, and he worried that Mom never got enough of a break. Neither did Cory, for that matter. Even though his friend didn't live here, he probably felt like it. It was the Hotel California of ranches—check out anytime you like, but you can never really leave.

Royce dropped the groceries inside his place, planning on putting everything away later. He grabbed a cold Coke from the fridge, since he still had hours of work ahead of him, and headed to the barn. He checked on Chevy, his very pregnant horse. She whinnied at him and shook out her dark mane. He gave her some grain, taking a minute to brush down her reddish-brown coat, even though he had a hundred other chores to attend to.

"What am I going to do?" Talking to his horse seemed to help him work out his problems, even if her only input was neighs and nudges that usually meant *Stop being so stingy with the food.* "I thought I'd catch up before the new group got here, but I'm still behind, and it's only gonna get worse." Since this batch of kids was brand-new and Mom was focused on getting to know them so she could see what they needed most, they weren't very good ranch hands yet. "And if that wasn't bad enough, now I get to worry about covering my ass before someone takes me to the cleaners and I lose everything my family's worked their entire lives for."

Royce ran his hand across Chevy's pregnant stomach— it wouldn't be long until she had her foal. It'd be good not only to have her baby, but also to have her back to working condition. He and Dad had spent countless hours together breaking and training her, and he could still remember the way they'd celebrated when they discovered that she went after cows faster than any gelding they'd ever had. They'd planned on raising her to be a broodmare because of her cowy nature and strong bloodline, but after Royce entered a couple of rodeos with her, she proved that she was born to rope.

Now they were both out of the roping scene for the most part, but she was still his best horse. Of course, she'd need time to recover, and the colt or filly would need training, too—which just brought him back to his current problem of needing another person to help. It was looking more and more like he might have to let some of the qualifications go and just find someone desperate for a job.

. . .

The instant Sadie stepped inside the house, Mom jumped up from the couch. As much complaining as she'd done over the phone about how old she was getting, she looked the same, not even a hint of gray creeping into her bright red hair. Sadie threw her arms around her, squeezing her tightly, then she leaned over to hug Grandma before she tried to get up from her chair. The silver lining in her currently broke-and-jobless situation was seeing her family. Earlier this spring Grandma had gotten pneumonia and been hospitalized for a couple of weeks. Sadie had been worried about her—they all had—but the strength with which she hugged Sadie gave her hope Grandma was well on her way to recovery.

Grandpa watched on, silent but smiling, and her heart swelled. It was funny how one minute she wanted to escape town, and the next she couldn't imagine leaving them again to live so far away.

Mom glanced from the suitcase Sadie had rolled in to the large duffel bag Grandpa had set down at the foot of the stairs. "Is that it?" She looked at it again, as if she might have missed a bag. "I know you said it was just temporary, but I expected more."

"I would've brought more if I had my car, but it was on its last legs and there was no way it'd make the drive, so I sold it. I put most of my belongings in storage." She didn't mention that she'd used every last penny to rent the storage space and buy the one-way plane ticket.

Having a singing contract in reaching distance—for the second time, no less—only to have it all fall apart again had drained the last of the fight in her. When she'd tried to get back on the horse—or stage, as it were—she'd only managed to crash harder. All she'd really been thinking when she'd called Mom and told her she was coming home to spend some time with her, Grandma, and Grandpa was that she *needed* to get away from Nashville and all of the pressure for a while. She'd be lying if she said running out of money didn't have a little something to do with it. She might've been able to get her old job back if she hadn't told her boss that she'd rather shovel horseshit than work for him when she'd quit. In hindsight, not the smartest way to go.

But she didn't think she could've gone back and made one more phone call for that company anyway. Dialing up random people and trying to convince them to take surveys they didn't want to was exhausting, she'd hated being inside during all the sunny hours of the day, and her boss was a jerk. She'd tried waitressing before, but she got distracted easily, started chatting and laughing with the customers instead of focusing on the food and her other tables, and ended up getting yelled at a lot, so it wasn't a good fit, either. Sure, there were probably other jobs she could try, but she was too burned-out. A couple months to recoup and get back into fighting shape—repair the layer of thick skin one needed to have in the music industry and get her confidence back—and then she'd call up her agent and tell him she was ready to perform and try to get auditions again.

"I'm sorry I didn't get to cleaning out your room," Mom said. "I simply ran out of time. I washed the bedding, though. It's in the dryer now."

Sadie wrapped an arm around Mom's shoulders. "Thanks. That's perfect."

"Dinner's in the oven," Grandma said, and at the suggestion of food, Sadie smelled something buttery and creamy. "I made your favorite brownies for dessert, too. I wanted to celebrate you coming home."

Sadie almost told Grandma that she couldn't eat the delicious brownies with the calorific fudge frosting. Or whatever meat she'd most likely breaded and fried, not to mention the vegetables she nearly always served creamed, which sort of defeated the healthy aspect. Sadie had been on a strict diet for years, and carbs were so not her friends. Her agent always pointed out that she needed to look marketable to keep up with the rest of the competition, and she was told whenever she gained a pound or two. If Nolan had his way, she'd have breast implants, too. She'd actually considered getting them, but in the end, she really thought it should be about her voice. Showed what she knew. Sure, there were hundreds of good singers out there, but she'd networked, taken lessons, spent years pursuing a career, and she could sing, damn it!

Exhaustion seeped in and her shoulders sagged. With any luck, she'd figure out a way to get her mojo back. First things first, she was dying for a shower, and then bring on the food, because eating her feelings sounded like a great way to take care of them right now. She excused herself and dragged her suitcase upstairs.

"Is she okay?" she heard Mom ask, even though she was clearly trying to whisper. But with Grandma and Grandpa being a little hard of hearing, it came out as more of a yell-whisper.

Was she okay? It was the million-dollar question, wasn't it?

"Seems okay," Grandpa said. "Ran into Royce at the grocery store, and I think that was hard."

Sadie groaned. They were already going to start speculating about her love life, and there was no doubt the entire town would be buzzing about it, too. Everyone had thought the rodeo star and the town's singing sensation— if you counted state fairs, rodeos, and ball games—were going to make it. While most everyone in Hope Springs had speculated on what exactly had happened to break them up right before Sadie left, none of them knew the truth as far as she could tell. The only person who knew everything was Quinn, and she was so loyal she'd take it to her grave. There were definitely whispers about how Sadie thought she was too good for the town, though. Yet another reason she'd only been home twice since she'd moved away, both super-short visits where she'd honed her hermit skills.

Sadie pushed into her bedroom. Or maybe she'd traveled through the wormhole again. It still looked like the bedroom from her high school memories. There were the red curtains she'd sewn in class, because yeah, that had been required in the high school curriculum in this town. When the curtains were closed, you could see how crooked they were at the bottom. Posters of famous country singers lined the wall. Faith Hill, Miranda Lambert, Carrie Underwood, and Keith Urban. That last one was up there because, yes, he was a good singer, but he was also nice to look at. He was still nice to look at, but nowadays, she was more of a Brantley Gilbert girl. How could she resist a male country singer with a bad boy look?

On the other side of the room were lots of pictures tacked to the wall, most of them of her and Royce. The two of them after one of his big rodeo wins, the time she'd sung at open mic night in a club in Casper, prom, posed together in their graduation robes. Each moment had been frozen in time, and now they served as a reminder of all the things that had gone wrong. She should've taken them down last time she was here, but she'd been depressed over how she'd almost signed a contract with a record label only for the band to break up. That was the first time her singing dreams had slipped through her fingers.

Sadie pushed her suitcase aside, sat on the floral, pillow-topped mattress stripped of its bedding, and flopped back on it. She wondered why Mom had never taken down the pictures and done something else with the room. It had been easy enough to avoid, since they'd often meet up for Christmases in Casper, where they'd get a nice hotel room and Sadie could spend the holidays with both her mom and grandparents and her dad and stepmom, who lived there. Somehow her parents had actually managed to have a civil divorce and were one of those broken-up couples who could still be in the same room as each other and be fine. Mom always said they'd just been too young. It was why she'd ingrained in Sadie career first, everything else could wait.

After seeing firsthand how hard Mom had to work to get through school while juggling a job, as well as being a single parent, Sadie understood why she felt so strongly about it. After all, Mom had done some modeling when she was younger and had even been offered a contract with an agency—a contract she'd given up to stay in Wyoming and get married. Now she worked long hours for little pay.

Sadie had sworn she wouldn't squander any opportunity that came her way—that she'd follow her singing dreams and make enough money doing what she loved so her mom wouldn't have to work anymore. Obviously that hadn't happened. *Yet.* Until it did, she refused to be a financial strain on her family. Especially since she knew it was hard enough for them to keep up on all the bills as it was, and that was before Grandma's trip to the hospital and all the extra medications she had to take now.

Sadie sat up, resolve filling her. The job hunt would start first thing tomorrow, no taking time to wallow. She wasn't even sure where to start looking for a job, but at this point, she was desperate enough she'd pretty much take anything.

Chapter Three

Sadie took her mug of coffee out the back door and headed to the corral that attached to the small barn. Grandpa used to run horses on a big spread of land—one hundred and twenty acres that had now been separated into plots and sold off one at a time, all but the twenty closest to the house. He'd sold most of the horses, too, but he'd kept two. Apollo, the dun, and Casanova, the black stallion. People still paid Grandpa to have their horses breed with Casanova, because he produced good foals.

Casanova came trotting over, and Sadie set down her coffee and threw over a few flakes of hay. "You get with any hot ladies lately?" she asked as she ran her hand down the horse's nose.

He leaned into her hand, and she scratched his cheek the way he liked.

"I hate to break it to you, but you're looking kind of old." Since she remembered when he was born, that made her feel a little old as well. Twenty-five was far from getting up there, but lately she'd been very aware of how many years had passed since she'd set out to become a singer. Being in a short-lived music group with two girls who were barely twenty had only made her more aware of her age. Their inexperience was probably why they cared more about fighting and the spotlight than just getting a record out so their careers could start.

Stupid girls. Wait till they've been trying for several years and they realize opportunities like that don't come along every day.

Sadie turned when she heard the back screen door close, and Grandpa nodded at her. "Mornin'. Getting close to afternoon, actually. I wasn't sure you were getting up today," he teased.

After working late shifts for the past few years, she thought being showered and dressed by ten a.m. was a bragworthy accomplishment. "Good morning."

Casanova whinnied at her for attention, and she scratched his cheek again.

"Where's Apollo?" Just as she was starting to worry that something had happened to the mare, she came trotting out of the barn, a sturdy fence between her and Casanova.

Grandpa threw the horses more hay, and Sadie picked her mug back up and took a sip. She glanced at the now-empty chicken coop, remembering all the times Grandma would send her to get eggs and the chickens would scratch and peck at her.

She gestured to the coop. "You ever miss them?"

"Do I miss those peckers?"

"Grandpa!" Sadie laughed. She'd gotten in trouble at

school for using that word, in addition to the many other colorful terms he'd taught her while she'd been helping him on the farm.

"Nah. Not at all, actually. Miss having more horses sometimes, though. Royce invites me to the ranch here and there so I can still play cowboy with him and Cory. I can't keep up, but it's nice of them to humor me."

She could picture Grandpa riding beside Royce, and while she was still irritated about how frustrating her ex was yesterday, warmth filled her chest. She knew how much Grandpa liked to get in some cowboy time. "I'm sure you do fine."

"I'm old and slow." He tossed in a couple more flakes of hay.

Sadie wanted to ask a hundred questions about Royce, but she wasn't sure she could handle the answers or what they'd do to her emotions. It wasn't a good subject to go into, especially not with Grandpa. Although her grandparents had always been supportive, she had a feeling they'd wondered what she was thinking running off to the big city to try to become famous. Mom had encouraged it, of course, but after Sadie had been in Nashville a few years, even she'd mentioned that maybe college was the way to go—just to have something to fall back on.

Between work and auditions and performances that didn't pay much but gave her "great exposure," she'd doubted she could fit in college. She'd explained that the first few years were more like an internship that'd eventually pay off, and it'd come so close to being true. Maybe this next time around she'd take classes on the side—somehow she'd fit it all in.

But now she was getting ahead of herself, the way she often did. "So, I was planning on going around town and applying for jobs today," she said to Grandpa. "Mind if I take the truck? Or do you need it?"

"Go right ahead. Keys are in the ignition." Of course they were. This was Hope Springs, where people weren't worried about locking their vehicles or taking their keys inside.

"Thanks, Grandpa." She gave him a quick kiss on his whiskered cheek and headed back through the house. She wiped off the bits of hay that had gotten on her frilly white button-down top and black slacks—she was probably overdressed for most of the jobs she'd be applying for, but she needed to make a good impression. *First* impressions were long gone, so she could only hope to sway someone into seeing that she was qualified, regardless of a résumé that claimed otherwise.

I've sung in front of large crowds and jaded record execs. I sang a Blue cover in front of their fans and all of the media outlets covering his induction to the Louisiana Music Hall of Fame. I can handle a few interviews in Small Town, USA.

• • •

Royce looked over the lined-up teens, five girls and six boys, ages fourteen through seventeen. This part was his least favorite, where it was more about showing tough love and laying ground rules, and he didn't know the kids well enough to relax his guard. He eyed the tall scrawny kid in the middle, who had his arms crossed and an exaggerated scowl on his face so he could show everyone how unhappy he was to be here. The other kids were still a little standoffish, but settling in. Elijah—who'd spat to call him Eli—had bad attitude written all over him, and he wasn't about to let it go.

Mom lifted her clipboard. "Eli, Addison, and Brady, you're team one. Your job today is to clean the cabins, then we'll take you over to the horses and introduce you, and tonight you'll peel the potatoes for dinner."

Eli rolled his eyes.

"Anyone who doesn't pull their weight gets extra chores," Royce said, directing the comment at the kid, who immediately clenched his jaw. "We'll check over the work, and if you don't do it right, you'll be redoing it. But if you do it fast—and you do a good job—you'll get time to go to the river later."

"Ooh, the river," the kid mumbled. "Yeah, that sounds fun."

Royce's patience was wearing thin, especially after the exhausting morning he'd already had, on top of the late night he'd pulled.

Mom must've seen it, because she stepped in front of him, handed out the rest of the chores to the other two groups, and dismissed them. For now, each group needed to be supervised. The last thing they needed was a fight breaking out or for one of them to get angry and try to tear the rooms apart. They'd had plenty of both through the years. Dad had been better at handling it. He was more patient than Royce would ever be. That familiar longing of missing his dad settled into his lungs. There were still some days when it was harder than others, and the beginning of a new session always brought on the harder ones.

Mom tucked her clipboard under her arm and gave him

a consoling smile. "It's always like this at first. They're a good group."

"That Eli kid worries me."

"He's a big grouchy pants, that's for sure."

"'Grouchy pants.' That the textbook term?"

Mom laughed. "He'll come around. I put him with Addison because I think he's got a crush on her, and she's feisty enough to deal with his crap and give it right back. She wants to go down to the river and explore, too, so she'll keep him in line."

Royce expected Mom to head off to check on the groups, but she turned to face him, and there was something about her expression that made his muscles tense. "What now?" he asked. "I don't think I can handle one more problem."

"I had to take Oscar to the vet this morning."

Relief flooded him that the problem wasn't as bad as he expected, although he knew Mom would be devastated if anything happened to her mangy cat, despite the fact that he was the most high-maintenance animal they had. "Is he okay?"

She waved a hand through the air. "Oh, yeah. I was worried because he's been all sluggish and sneezy and goopy eyed. Doc said he's got a respiratory infection, so he'll have to be on antibiotics—not to mention he'll be pissed off at me for days for taking him in. But that's not why I brought it up. While I was there, I just heard that"—she wobbled her head, and apprehension crept into his gut—"Sadie's back in town."

Royce let out an exhale. "I know. I ran into her last night, actually."

"And…?"

"And nothing. I saw her, we…" He didn't want to tell Mom they'd argued, and that made it sound like a bigger deal than it was, anyway. "We just said hi and went our separate ways." Sadie's wide green eyes came to him again. He glanced toward the hills, doing his best to keep the talk casual. "They said she's back, back? Like going to stay?"

"Sounds like she'll be here for a while, anyway."

Dammit. He could wait out a visit—it wasn't like he went into town all the time. But if she were going to be here for more than a week or so, it'd be impossible to avoid her.

It doesn't matter, he told himself. *I moved on from that girl years ago.* Only his insides felt like they'd been tied in a knot, and little moments from their past were flashing through his mind again like a happy forgotten slide show.

He focused on the end of their relationship, on the night she'd told him she couldn't marry him. A week later she was gone, almost as if his question had caused her to flee as fast as possible. And now everyone in town was going to be buzzing about it, stopping him to ask what he thought of Sadie being back, watching every word and movement so they could add it to their theories, and he didn't have time for that.

He rubbed the back of his stiff neck. "Well, I've got to get to work."

Mom nodded, took a step toward the cabins, then abruptly stopped. "It was hard enough to find the time to drive Oscar into town, but since we're shorthanded, and I still need to have individual meetings with each kid, I was hoping you could maybe pick him up?"

He hadn't even broken the news to her about how she was practically legally bound to stay on the land until he found help, and he didn't want to unless he absolutely *had* to. "You just want him to scratch and bite me instead of you," he teased. The cat was named Oscar after Oscar the Grouch, and he lived up to his name.

Mom smiled. "Sometime before the clinic closes, which is five thirty."

"I'll squeeze it in. I've been meaning to see if anyone from the office wants a side job anyway. Maybe that'd be enough help to get us by for now. In the meantime, we can make Mister Bad Attitude clean out the stalls. Maybe shit shoveling will teach him some manners."

Mom pointed a warning finger. "One, you owe a dollar to the swear jar, and two, you be nice and give the kid a chance."

Royce shook his head but couldn't help cracking a smile. Mom and her swear jar. And her belief that there was a nice shiny person inside everyone, even if you had to dig to find it. Admittedly, he had seen a lot of pretty miraculous transformations, but there were a few now and then who left with the chips on their shoulders still fully intact, mostly because they absolutely refused to engage. "Yeah, yeah. I'm sure we'll be great buds by the end of his stint." Maybe if he ever got enough sleep that his patience wasn't so stretched thin it was practically nonexistent, it'd help.

Still, sometimes he thought he was the worst possible choice to be in charge of the camp.

• • •

"Sadie Hart, is that really you?"

Sadie barely restrained herself from dropping the swear

word on the tip of her tongue. You know the type of girls who make high school miserable? Who turn everything into a competition and manage to insult you but make it seem like they don't realize it's an insult? Well, the pretty brunette staring at her was one of those girls.

"Gracie Walker. Hey."

"I heard you were back in town." The twangy accent was thick with this one. "Whatever happened to Nashville? Last I heard, you were part of some cute girl band."

See? An insult wrapped in a package with a big ol' bullshit bow. "I'm back home for a while."

"So you've given up on the singing thing? That's a shame. I remember all those times you sang the national anthem. I bet they'll let you perform again at the ball games and such. You better ask real quick about the Fourth of July rodeo, 'cause it's comin' up pretty soon, and they might've already booked someone else."

This was her ninth—or was it tenth?—stop. Most of them had gone about like this, with slightly less passive-aggressiveness. She'd filled out several applications and handed out résumés, even though everyone had claimed they weren't hiring. When she'd stopped at the diner to eat lunch, she'd asked there, too, but they told her they weren't in need of any more waitresses, even part-time. Considering how much she sucked at waitressing, that was probably for the best.

So she'd wandered into the bank, and now she wished she'd just skipped it. Gracie had never liked her much because she'd always had a thing for Royce. It was funny how that determined a girl not liking her, even all these years later when she wasn't even with him. In fact, she was almost sure Gracie was married now. She wanted to ask if they could just grow up and get over it, but she really, really needed a job, so she put on a sugary smile. "Yeah, maybe I'll get lucky and they'll have me back." *And eventually, I'll get a recording contract and make you eat your words.* "Before that, though, I need a job. Who would I talk to about the openings here?"

"That'd be me."

"Great." *Damn it!* "Do you have any openings? I'm willing to start at the bottom and work my way up. I'm great with customers, have lots of experience directing calls, and—"

"We're all filled up right now. In fact, we just had to downsize. The last person we let go had been here for three years."

This morning's pep talk was a distant memory, and everything inside of her just sort of deflated. "Can I fill out an application in case something opens up?"

Gracie looked like she was about to say no, but Sadie must've looked as desperate as she felt, because her old nemesis pursed her lips and slid a paper across the desk. "You can take it, fill it out, and then just drop it back by next time you come this way."

"Thanks."

Sadie took the application and stumbled out of the bank, lifting her hand to shield her eyes from the cornea-piercing sunshine. She wanted to kick off her shoes, sit down in the middle of the sidewalk, and call it quits. From the looks of things, there wasn't an open job in all of Hope Springs. Apparently she needed to wait for someone to retire or die before she got a job. What a nice, cheery thought.

If I wait for that to happen, I'll just end up stuck here for years, my contacts and opportunities all dried up, and I can't let that happen. I'm just going to have to convince someone—anyone—to give me a job.

She spotted the Hope Springs Animal Clinic and figured she could try one more place before quitting for the day. Big breath in, chin up, a confident expression and…go.

The second she stepped inside, her breath shot out of her, her mouth dropped, and her confidence fell in a puddle on the floor.

"…guess I'll just pick up the cat then," Royce said, and one of the two girls working the front desk turned and disappeared into the back.

It was worse than she'd expected, the inability to go anywhere without running into him. He seemed even larger in here than he had at the grocery store. Maybe it was his black cowboy hat, the dirty jeans that made it clear he'd worked all day, or his booted feet casually crossed at the ankle as he leaned his tall frame on the counter. Talk about the perfect image of a cowboy. At least she looked better than she had last night, although walking around in the heat all day had probably left her a little crumpled-looking.

"Can I help you?" the girl behind the desk asked.

Royce glanced over his shoulder. The smile died on his lips.

Oh my gosh, he haaates me.

"Miss Sadie?"

Sadie turned her attention to the girl behind the desk. She looked so familiar, but it took a couple of seconds to put together the pieces now that the braces were gone and her long hair was dyed blond instead of the brown shade it used to be. "Brianna?"

The girl Sadie used to babysit came from behind the desk and hugged her—they'd played Candy Land and colored in books filled with cartoon characters. Royce had even come over a few times while Sadie was babysitting. And here they all were standing in a circle.

So freaking weird.

"Guess what, I'm engaged now!" Brianna thrust her hand and diamond-banded finger in Sadie's face.

And the weird just. Kept. Coming. "Wow!"

"Yeah, to Dusty Brooks."

Cory's little brother. Sadie automatically glanced at Royce, but his gaze was focused on a spot on the wall, even though there were only pictures of animals, and he couldn't be *that* interested in the "Hang in There" poster with the cat barely clinging to a branch.

Oh, kitty, believe me, I'm trying, but I'm about to slip right off.

"Wow," Sadie said again, because she didn't know what else to say.

"Dusty competes at rodeos now, the way Royce used to. He's getting really good, and people all around the state know who he is."

Royce's jaw tightened. Sadie wasn't sure if it was caused by regret that he didn't compete in the rodeo circuit anymore, or if he was just that annoyed by her presence. She had the oddest urge to reach out and squeeze his hand. Years ago, it would've been the most natural thing in the world, but now…

Well, now he'd probably jerk away and tell her to never touch him again.

The girl who'd disappeared into the back brought out

a small carrier and set it on the counter. The cat inside was growling and attacking the bars.

"Poor little thing." Sadie peered into the carrier. Whoa. Not so little after all. A big gray poofball with yellow-green eyes. "You're gonna be all right, kitty cat."

"That's Oscar the Grouch," Brianna offered.

"He's less green and unibrowed than I remember."

Royce gave a sort of snort-laugh, then his eyes met hers, and it was like he forced himself to put on a scowl again. *Speaking of grouches.*

Sadie reached her finger toward the metal squares of the carrier.

"He'll bite you," Royce said, but she ignored him, using her most soothing voice to tell the cat about how she'd be grouchy, too, if she were poked and prodded and shoved in a box. As soon as her finger hit his chin, he calmed and started to purr, rubbing up against the bars to get closer.

"So, Sadie." Brianna settled into her chair and reached for her computer mouse. "Did you need to make an appointment?"

Sadie straightened, trying not to let the fact that she was suddenly sweating like crazy show. She didn't want to say anything in front of Royce, but it looked like that wasn't an option. "Actually, I'm lookin' for a job and hoped you had an opening. I'm good with animals and—"

"No jobs here, I'm afraid, but Royce was just saying he's looking for someone to help out at Second Chance Ranch."

"Oh, no," Sadie said at the same time Royce said, "It wouldn't be a good job for her."

They stared at each other for a beat, awkwardness crowding the space between them. Underneath the weirdness, though, anger was also rising up, and she'd never been good at biting her tongue. "What do you mean, it wouldn't be a good job for me?"

"You said no."

"Well, yeah, but…"

He crossed his arms, and seriously, when did he get a chest like that? And those muscled cords in his forearms. And was it hot in here? "But what?"

Good-looking and well built or not—and he definitely was—he was the most infuriating person she'd ever met. Thank goodness she hadn't actually married him.

Instead of the satisfaction that thought should've brought, an icy lump formed in her stomach.

She ran her hand across her forehead and turned to Brianna. "If any job comes up—anything at all—please call." She placed a card on the desk, even though it said she was a singer, which wasn't totally true these days. It still had her cell number on it, anyway. "And congratulations again on your engagement."

She spun and walked out of the office, thinking about how crazy it was that people as young as Dusty and Brianna were already engaged. Around here, though, it wasn't uncommon for people to get hitched shortly after high school. In fact, it was the norm, and it wasn't like they were getting married because the girl was knocked up or anything—though that usually followed pretty quickly, and there were, of course, plenty of cases of that happening. Sure, there were a few holdouts who waited until their thirties, which was somehow considered old and usually created gossip about whether or not he or she would ever settle down. And while there was the occasional divorce, most marriages around here stuck.

I so *don't belong here*, Sadie thought as she walked back down the sidewalk as fast as she could in her heels, needing to hop into Grandpa's truck and escape not only her failure to get any job leads, but also the angry expression on her ex's face that seemed to be seared into her brain.

• • •

Royce watched Sadie's retreating figure out the window. Back in the day, he'd chase her down and tell her he was sorry, like the whipped fool he was. If she thought he was still a pushover, though, she was wrong.

"That was pretty crazy how she tamed the cat like that, huh?" Brianna pushed a clipboard toward him. "He's what we call fractious, which means he's uncooperative and unruly, and we always have to sedate him when he's in here. I've never seen him calm."

"Maybe you should hire her, then."

"I know Dr. Jones isn't looking for help, but I'll still mention it." She handed him the bag with the antibiotics and instructions for the cat, then pointed at the bottom of the paper on the clipboard. "Sign here, please."

Royce scribbled his name and took the now-hissing-and-growling cat to his truck and set the carrier next to him on the seat. If he stuck his finger through the bars, he had no doubt Oscar would bite the hell out of him.

He closed his eyes and all he could see was Sadie. Today she'd had on red lipstick that brought out her full lips. Lips he used to be addicted to. Royce groaned, annoyed and semi-turned on all at the same time. How could she still do that to him so easily? Once in a while over the years, yes, she'd crossed his mind. A song that came on the radio would remind him of her, or a memory would come out of the blue and smack into him. But now that he was seeing her every day… She always did have this way of mesmerizing people. And it only got worse when she sang—or better, depending on which way you looked at it.

He fired up his truck and headed back toward the ranch. As he drove, he couldn't help remembering the first time he'd heard her sing. Sadie Hart had transferred to Hope Springs High during their sophomore year. Her parents had gotten divorced and she and her mom had moved in with her grandparents. Of course he'd noticed her on her first day of school—she was new, and she was hot. But she'd immediately started dating Forrest Scott, one of the cocky running backs on the football team. While Royce kicked himself for not acting sooner, he was competing in a lot of rodeos and cute girls flirted with him all the time, so he'd decided to enjoy being single.

But then the Fourth of July rodeo came around and Sadie stepped up to the microphone to sing the national anthem. Moments before, he'd been focused on the upcoming roping event, just wanting to fast-forward to when he was on Chevy and swinging a lasso through the air. After that, he'd have to quickly shift gears to get his head right for bronc riding. The second she opened her mouth and sang that first note, though, he stood there at the edge of the arena, under her spell with the rest of the crowd. She belted out the song with so much soul he'd felt it in his—he'd never heard anyone sound that amazing a cappella, and he'd been to his fair share of rodeos, across several states. As she finished off the song, he thought, *Holy shit, I think I'm in love.*

He'd happened to be near the gate she was coming out of, so he tipped his hat at her and said, "That was real good."

Her full lips curved into a heart-stopping smile, and she clamped onto his arm. "Really? I was so nervous when they handed me the microphone that I thought I was going to ralph, and I was totally regretting scarfing half a pizza earlier. Dude, I'm still shaking." She gave a nervous laugh and then looked him over, her eyes slowly coming back to his. "Hey, good luck on the cowboy thing tonight. I'll be cheering for you."

And that was it. He was a goner.

So he started talking to her every chance he got—she had this infectious laugh that lit up her eyes, and she also did this shoulder-bump thing every time he cracked a joke. She was funny and quick, always with a comeback when most people never even got that he wasn't being serious. Unfortunately, she was still with Forrest.

The day he found out they'd broken up, Royce strode up to her and said, "Go out with me."

She turned to him, her eyes going wide. "Royce, I just—"

"Broke up with Forrest. I know. So go out with me. Dinner. Movie. Dancing. You pick. I'll be at your house tomorrow night at seven and you can tell me then." He walked away before she could say no, and his nerves were tangling themselves up in his gut.

But when he glanced over his shoulder, she was staring after him, and he knew that he'd never be the same again.

He'd been right. Just not in the way he'd expected.

Chapter Four

Going through these pictures was torture. She should rip them down without looking. Why was she studying each one?

But she couldn't stop.

For one, she'd been forced to pass them by a dozen times over the last few days, and she was sick of it. Two, she didn't have a job or anything else to do, and three—and really, it was the main reason—she looked so blissfully happy in all of them. The few months after she'd moved to Nashville had been hard. She'd missed home and had found herself halfway through dialing Royce's number on several occasions. Each time, she'd force herself to stop and go out with her new roommates—there's no moving on when you're still holding on to the past, and she knew hearing his voice would completely undo any progress she'd made.

Eventually, it got easier. The city was alive, events happening day and night; she'd met great people and started booking singing gigs. She was doing what she loved and, before long, it became home. Lately, though, she'd had to put on a lot of fake smiles, even during some of her auditions. Once she started singing and everything else faded away, they'd turn genuine, because when she was performing and tingly energy wound through her, all that existed was her and the song.

But the picture version of Sadie was the kind of happy that looked like she was in on some big joke. Then there were the pictures where she was looking at Royce like he was the only thing in the world that mattered.

As she ran her eyes across the picture of them, him in his Wranglers, his too-big jacket draped over her, noses so close they almost touched, she remembered what it was like being Royce Dixon's girl.

She'd noticed him her first day at Hope Springs High—how couldn't she? But he'd hardly talked to her, unlike Forrest, who'd showered her with attention and had been her first boyfriend here. Once she started talking to Royce, though, she'd learned that underneath the steely, badass cowboy shell was an amazing guy who was quick-witted and had a soft spot for his family and his horse. They'd quickly become friends, and she developed a wicked crush—even though she was still with Forrest.

The second she was single, Royce had asked her out, and she knew she didn't stand a chance at a respectable period between relationships. She'd heard people talk about electricity and butterflies; being with Royce was like a lightning storm and hummingbirds. She'd actually gasped the first time he'd pressed his lips to hers. Then he'd enveloped her in his arms, deepened the kiss, and made her forget anything else existed.

No wonder the Sadie in the picture is smiling. She was experiencing the best relationship of her life. As pissed as she was at the younger girls for squabbling and dissolving the band she used to be in, she couldn't really talk. She'd let a good thing slip between her fingers before, too.

The knock on her door made her jump, and the pictures in her hand slipped to the floor, scattering in all different directions. Memories she'd have to pick back up and relive all over again.

Mom walked in, wearing her Mickey Mouse scrubs. She worked for the local pediatrician, who was, embarrassingly enough, still Sadie's doctor. She'd never seen any reason to change, what with Mom working there and all. Well, unless it was time for a gyno visit. Then she traveled as far as possible, since awkward run-ins with someone who'd examined down there would be highly likely anytime she went for a stroll through town.

"I need you to take the quilting stands back to Caroline, along with a pie I baked for her as a thank-you for letting me borrow them. And Grandpa wrote Royce a check for the hay and set it by the pie, so make sure you get that, too."

Sadie stared at Mom for a moment, waiting for her to say, *Just kidding!* After the longest pause ever, it was clear she wasn't going to. "Caroline Dixon? You want me to drive out to Second Chance Ranch and talk to Royce and his mom?"

"Grandpa took Grandma to Salt Lake to check out ovens at Lowe's, and I've got to go to work. But the quilting stands are already loaded into the back of the truck, thanks to your grandpa."

Part of her couldn't believe her grandparents were driving a couple hours to Utah just to go to a home improvement store, and the other part of her was sad they hadn't taken her. She always took the city for granted until it was far away. "Can't it wait? And who even writes checks these days? I couldn't find my checkbook if I tried."

Mom crossed her arms and raised an eyebrow.

"Fine. I'll take care of it. This isn't some attempt you and Caroline cooked up to get me and Royce talking, is it?"

"Yes, I run around like a crazy person with no time so that you have to face your ex-boyfriend."

Clearly, her love of sarcasm had been inherited from Mom—that and the strawberry hue in her hair when it was au naturel were about all she'd inherited from her. They'd never been the type to sit down to have heart-to-hearts. Part of that was because Mom was always so busy, but it sometimes felt like they just didn't speak the same language, which in turn, often left Sadie upset at Dad for moving on so easily, sending a check in his place, as if that'd make up for his absence in her life.

Luckily, Sadie had always had a connection with Grandpa, and she'd spent hours sitting with Grandma, who'd always listen and then chime in with great advice, so if anything she had more parents instead of fewer after the divorce.

That, as well as becoming friends with Quinn, and eventually Royce, had changed her perspective from thinking moving here was the tragedy she'd first thought it was. The friends she'd made in Nashville were fun to hang out with but not great with the deeper stuff, and she missed having people around whom she could share everything with.

Mom wound her hair into a bun. "I'll be off around six. There's chicken thawing, so if you wanna start peeling potatoes about a quarter till, that'd be a great help. Then we'll fry up the chicken and make gravy. Oh and there's a load of clothes in the washer, but I ran out of time, so switch them to the dryer for me, okay?

"Thanks," she said without waiting for an answer, then pressed a quick kiss to Sadie's forehead and rushed out of the room, leaving her with that same dropped-through-the-wormhole feeling. It really was like high school all over again. Sadie didn't mind helping—in fact, it'd be nice to have something to do—but she wondered why Mom would ask Grandpa if she was okay, but not her. They hadn't even talked about what had happened with her contract falling through, or how after that, she'd choked and screwed up her only other steady gig.

She gathered the pictures from the floor and hovered them over the trash can but couldn't drop them in for reasons she didn't care to think about right now. So she stuck the stack on the back of the dresser, out of sight. Unfortunately, that made her face her reflection. She hadn't bothered with makeup or even changing out of her pajamas yet.

Yikes! Not going to the ranch looking like this.

At least this time, she'd get to prepare herself before seeing Royce. She shimmied into her tightest jeans—one of the Miss Me pairs with the rhinestones on the pockets that she was obsessed with—threw on a white tank top and a filmy purple blouse, and pulled on the way-too-expensive boots she'd gotten when she thought she'd landed a record deal. The boots were all looks, no function, but a little dust wouldn't hurt them.

After curling her hair in uniform waves, she switched over the laundry. Then she grabbed the pie, check, and truck keys and drove the familiar road to Second Chance Ranch.

This year was a bit dry, the grass browner than usual, which both Royce and Grandpa had no doubt worried about. With each mile closer she got to the ranch, her heart beat a little faster, and her grip on the steering wheel tightened that much more. The wooden sign over the entrance was new, done in the same print as the sign on the door of Royce's truck. The quilting stands in the back bumped together as she took the turn.

Sadie caught movement behind the cabins where the teens stayed, so she pulled up next to the nearest one, took a deep breath, and got out of the truck.

She was sidetracked when she saw a familiar figure filling the water trough. Since going to say hi to Cory would be much easier than seeing Royce, she chose to start with him. She walked over and tapped his shoulder, grinning when he did a double take.

He scooped her into a hug. "Hey! I heard you were in town."

"You heard right," she said, squeezing him back. Then she stepped away and looked him over. Same deep dimples set in tan skin, piercing blue eyes, and jet-black hair peeking out from under a beat-up cowboy hat. The thick, dark scruff was new, though, and like Royce, he'd filled out quite a bit since high school.

The hug had knocked his hat crooked, and he readjusted it with one hand on top, wiggling it back into place. "So, how've you been, big shot? I guess I better get an autograph before I lose my chance."

"Oh, you're definitely not at risk of that. As you might've noticed, I'm not exactly a big shot yet. And even if I were, you know I'd always have time for you." She flashed him a smile, glad that despite all the time away, things were still easy between them. "It's been an interesting few years, though. Ups and downs and everything in between, but I've managed to hold my own. How about you? How's life?"

"Good, good. Playing cowboy. Same old."

Not exactly *playing* from the looks of things. She bet he was still a total heartbreaker, too—he had Native American somewhere in his bloodline, and between his coloring, those blue eyes, and the natural good ol' boy charm, the girls went crazy for him.

The water spilled over the side of the trough, and Cory moved to shut it off. "Hey, I gotta go hop on a tractor before it gets too dark, but let's catch up later, okay?"

"Sure," she said, though she doubted there'd be a later. It'd be too weird to meet up without Royce, and she couldn't picture them all sitting around like old times. "Is Royce or Caroline around?"

"They're both behind the cabins with the kids."

She nodded, delaying the inevitable for a moment, but when Cory took off, she forced her feet into motion. As she made her way to the shared backyard of the camp cabins, she spotted a bunch of teens holding ropes. Royce was in the middle of the action, teaching one of the guys to lasso. She could tell he was explaining the movement and the feel, like he had with her all those years ago, when she'd asked him to teach her.

It was amazing watching him from this perspective. He was so patient, laughing it off when the guy missed and giving him a pat on the back as he handed the kid the rope to try again. He moved to the girl standing next in line and started taking her through the steps. There was a tall, dark-haired kid in back with his arms crossed and a scowl on his face.

Now that just wouldn't do. She'd seen the change this place made in kids' lives before, but sometimes they needed an extra push, and cheering up grumpy people was one of the things besides singing that she did well. Sadie slowly moved over to him. "What? You're too cool for this stuff?"

He turned toward her, and she was sure he was about to let her have it, but then his mouth just sort of hung open. "I…uh…yeah."

She flashed him the grin she'd used in waitressing to win over people when she accidentally messed up their orders—she'd had to use it a *lot*. "When I first moved here, I thought it was lame, too." But then she'd seen Royce doing it, and it was different in competition, when the entire crowd leaned forward, waiting to see if the throw would land. "Where are you from?"

"Fort Collins, Colorado." He crossed his arms and the attitude crept back in, his lips pursed together.

"And your name?"

"Eli. You gonna ask me why I'm here, too?"

"Only if you ask me first. Trust me, this is the *last* place I expected to be."

That earned her half a smile.

"I'm Sadie." She eyed the discarded rope at his feet. "You want me to show you how to rope? I learned way back when, and I kind of suck, so don't show me up after I teach you, 'kay?"

Eli rolled his eyes and sighed, but she picked up the rope anyway and bumped her shoulder into his. "Come on. What else are you gonna do?"

"Fine. But it's still lame."

"Not if you think about the most annoying people you know and imagine you're roping them and jerking them off their feet." She gripped the knot—the honda, she remembered—fed the rope through, and flipped the loop back, repeating the move until it was about armpit height, the way she'd been taught by Royce. "I don't want to give names, because chances are you might run into her, but there was this snotty girl in high school—you know the type?"

"Sure. Know lots of them."

"So you just picture them…" Sadie gripped the loop and lifted it above her head. "You swivel your wrist and—" The rope smacked her on the side of the head, but she was already trying to throw.

It landed on the ground in front of her, not even coming close to the bale with the plastic cow head stuck into it. "Shit."

Eli laughed. "You do suck."

"Hey." She gave him a playful shove. "I said *kind of*."

"Oh, and there's a swear jar, and you need to put a dollar in it."

"Seriously? A swear jar?"

"It's bullshit, right?"

"I'm so telling on you," she said with a laugh, and he laughed again.

• • •

What the hell?

Royce stared across the yard at Sadie and Eli. First of all, what was she even doing here, and second, how did she get that kid to laugh?

She glanced up and her eyes met his. Her smile faded and she swallowed. Was he really that scary? Realizing he was frowning at them, he worked to soften his expression and walked over.

"Sadie."

"Royce."

Eli glanced between them. "I'll just…" He pointed toward the other kids. "I think I need a new teacher anyway."

"Oh, sure, I let one little bale of hay get away, and you think I don't know what I'm doing?" She threw her hand over her heart. "That hurts."

Damn if the kid didn't smile at her again before heading away.

"How'd you do that?" Royce asked.

"I'm just a little rusty, and you know I was never good at roping anyway. I always secretly cheered for the calves to get away. Not when you were competing, of course, because I wanted you to win, but—"

"I'm not talking about the roping—although I really did think I taught you better than that." He'd only seen the end of the throw, if you could even call it that.

She raised a haughty eyebrow, one corner of her mouth hinting at a smile, and now he was thinking about her confession that she'd cheered for the calves and trying not to be amused by it. Not that it was a big surprise. In high school he'd repeatedly assured her all the animals at the rodeos were well taken care of, and she'd often chased calves down to try to pet them like overgrown puppies. He resisted the urge to tease her more, because that'd only lead down a road he wasn't going with her again.

He jerked his chin toward Eli. "I'm talking about the kid." While her ability to make people happy was something he'd seen—and experienced—before, getting through to someone that hell-bent on being angry was a whole new level.

"Eli? Seems like a good guy."

Good guy? Really? He narrowed his eyes at her, trying to see if she was serious. She stared right back, and he could see her jaw clench, the stubbornness setting in right in front of his eyes.

"I've never seen him smile before today," Royce said. "I was starting to wonder if he knew how."

She shrugged a shoulder, a smug quirk to her lips. "What can I say? People love me."

Royce took off his hat and ran a hand through his hair before replacing it and pulling the brim low. People loved her. Angry cats loved her.

"Sadie!" Mom's voice was about a hundred octaves higher than usual. She ran over and threw her arms around Sadie.

Moms loved her.

They spoke quickly, right over the top of each other. His mom was fawning over Sadie, telling her how happy she was to see her. It was borderline annoying, actually, but it—along with what had just happened with Eli—was giving him a horrible, awful idea.

"…wanted me to bring back your quilting stands, and she made a pie, too." Sadie glanced at him and swiped her hair behind her ear. "And I have a check for you from my grandpa."

"Well, let's go get the stands." Royce called for the kids to help, and they all walked toward the truck. It didn't take them long to load them into his mom's place, and big surprise, the rest of the teens took a shine to Sadie, too. For the most part, the kids sent here were just a bit misguided and used to people treating them like troublemakers. Pretty soon, they started shutting out all adults and living up to the name. One of the hardest things about finding someone to work with them was getting the right mix of tough love and respect.

Right now I'd settle for respect and the ability to get through to them, though…

He told the kids they could have some free time, Mom disappeared along with them, and then it was just him and Sadie, her at the bottom of the porch stairs and him at the top.

She kicked at the ground with her fancy boots. "So, um, I noticed you've got wifi now," she said, gesturing to the sign in the window of the cabins that reminded the kids they could have internet time on the community computer if they completed their chores. "Fancy."

"Yeah, and we stopped churning butter just last month. Super excited about it."

She shot him a scowl, and man, she was cute when she was mad, something he really wished he didn't notice. They say it takes about a month to break a habit, but even after all these years, he had to fight the urge to pull her into his arms and find a way to wipe the frown from her face.

He gripped the porch railing over his head to make sure

he didn't accidentally try it. Then he stared at her for a beat, telling himself not to say anything besides good-bye. All those thoughts about her people skills were just that, and they needed to stay locked away. "So, did you find a job?"

She gave a humorless laugh. "Not so much. I filled out a bunch of applications, but apparently no one in the town is hiring—working fast food is starting to look like my only option. I'm probably going to have to swallow my pride and fill out applications for that next week."

He pictured her behind the counter of McDonald's. He thought it would give him a sense of satisfaction. Instead, it felt like a lead weight in his gut. She didn't belong there, and she hated to be cooped up indoors. "I'm hiring."

"Funny."

Holy shit, what was he doing? But at this point, he was desperate, not to mention severely sleep deprived, and he couldn't seem to stop. "I'm serious. I've been shorthanded for a couple of months, and with the new batch of kids here for the alternative camp, it's even worse. I need someone who knows how to work with the teens and with animals, and is willing to do other chores around the ranch."

She was also female, something his eyes were taking in despite his best efforts to not check her out—another habit he'd apparently failed to break. He cleared his throat and forced his gaze to her face. "You remember how to take care of horses?"

She scrunched up her eyebrows, suspicion clear on her features. "Better than I remember how to rope. But why would you offer me a job?"

Yeah, why, Dixon? Why'd you have to go and open your big mouth? And if she accepted, could he really handle seeing her every day? Then again, could he afford to go another day without her here, helping balance out the gender equation?

He let go of the porch railing and leaned against one of the posts. "Sure, us working together is probably the worst idea ever, but you connected with Eli in record time, you're good with animals, and I'd get a kick out of seeing if you can still handle a little manure on your clothes or if you're too prissy now." He shrugged. "Plus, I give you a week. Two, tops."

"A week?" She crossed her arms. "Do you not remember how stubborn I can be if I set my mind to something?"

"I remember. It's another reason I'm offering you the job. Pay's not great and the hours are long, but if you think you can handle—"

"I'll take it."

"I'll see you tomorrow at seven a.m., then. You might wanna wear something a little more practical." And hopefully something that wouldn't show off the fact that while she was far too skinny now, she still had a nice butt.

She lifted her chin. "Great. See you then." She turned and strode to her truck, those damn rhinestones on her back pockets glittering in the sunshine with each sway of her hips.

And Royce knew he'd just done the dumbest thing in the history of dumb.

Chapter Five

The next morning, hours before she usually woke up, Sadie pulled up to Second Chance Ranch once again. She had no idea what to expect. She wouldn't be surprised if Royce laughed in her face and told her he'd only been joking about the job.

She was actually ten minutes early, and she wasn't sure if she should sit in the truck or go ask what jobs needed started, or what. After a moment of listening to silence so loud it was unnerving, she walked up to the large cabin that hadn't been there back in high school. Thanks to Grandpa telling her about how Royce and his dad were building it the first time she'd come back home for a visit, she knew it was his.

Maybe I should knock on Caroline's door instead. She glanced at the cabin about twenty yards over, then back at Royce's door. *Stop being a wimp and let's get this job started.*

She knocked on the door so hard it stung her knuckles, especially with the morning chill that wouldn't burn off for an hour or so.

Just when she'd decided he wasn't going to answer, the door swung open. Royce squinted against the morning light. His hair was sticking up in several places, and his shirt was unbuttoned, exposing a strip of his chest and stomach, muscles achieved through hard days on the farm instead of hours at the gym. She couldn't explain exactly what the difference was, but there definitely was one, and it ignited a spark of desire she hadn't felt in a long time.

She'd managed to sidestep memories of the sex they used to have, but now they lured her in. Blips of pleasure in rapid succession. His hands traveling over her body, kisses that merged into one another, the contrast of the warmth between their entwined bodies with the cool night air.

Royce cleared his throat, and she quickly looked up to his face. Heat burned through her cheeks. "Um, I'm…" She rubbed the back of her neck, which was also too warm now. "I was just wondering…"

"Coffee's almost done. Come on in, and you can have a cup. Maybe it'll help with the rambling problem."

She clamped her lips, sure her face was bright red, and followed him inside. She glanced up at the vaulted ceiling with the thick wooden beams and then at the large, open room. The dark wood of the furniture contrasted the lighter shade of the ceiling and walls. It was all masculine elegance, but not as rustic as she'd expected. Massive windows overlooked the ranch, there was a beautiful stone fireplace in the middle, and the room had red accents all around.

"Wow, Royce. This place is beautiful."

He turned to her, fastening the top button of his shirt—no more peep show, dang it. He swept his gaze over the room and then gave a tiny nod. "Thanks. It took my dad and me a few years to get it all done…" She could see the sadness flicker through his eyes, but he quickly shuttered it away. "But it's nice to have a place of my own, even if my mom's still my closest neighbor. Well, her and a bunch of juvenile delinquents."

He said it lightly, and it was clear that he had a soft spot for the supposed juvenile delinquents. Sadie took a step toward him. "I'm so sorry about your dad." When she'd heard he'd had a heart attack, she could hardly believe it. He was so young still. "He was such a great guy, and the world was a better place because of him." She knew her words were too little too late, but she had to get them out. Royce had always been close to his dad. He'd never been embarrassed to have him around, and they'd gone camping and hunting, as well as worked tireless hours together, and she knew he must've taken the loss hard.

He met her eyes, just for a beat, and his throat worked a swallow. "Thanks."

She wanted to ask more, dig deeper to see how he really was dealing with it, but he quickly turned away, making it clear she wouldn't get more than that. It wasn't just his dad, either—she could see the stress hanging on him, and she wanted to know what had him so worried. But she knew it wasn't her place anymore. Would never be again.

Her heart gave a sharp squeeze as past sorrow rose to the surface. Doing her best to shove it back down, she followed Royce as he continued to the kitchen. Dark granite countertops met pale wood, and all the appliances were black. Royce filled two mugs of coffee. He poured cream in one, added two spoonfuls of sugar, and slid it across to her.

Warmth spread through her chest. *He remembers how I*

like my coffee.

She sipped from her mug and he did the same. She kept wanting to say something, then second-guessing herself, and so they just drank in silence. The only time they'd had silence between them when they dated was when they were making out, only their labored breaths between them. Her gaze moved to his lips. Of all the guys she'd kissed, he blew everyone else out of the water. Other guys were sloppy or too ambitious with their tongues. He'd perfected the kiss.

Not to mention how perfect other things were, too. She used to wonder if she were weird, because while several of her girlfriends complained about their boyfriends wanting sex all the time, she'd craved the feel of Royce's skin against hers. Used to count down the hours until they could sneak away alone. She'd never had that same intense connection with anyone else—not by a long shot.

He took the mug from her hands even though she wasn't quite done and set it in the sink. "Let's start with the horses."

• • •

The woman needed to stop undressing him with her eyes. He'd almost crushed the mug in his hand when she'd licked her lips while staring at him.

His head got that the girl was dangerous, so why did his body respond in all the wrong ways? He took a deep breath to lower his heart rate and headed outside, not looking back to see if she was following.

When they got to the stables, he started the rundown. "About half of the horses are pasture fed right now, but we're boarding ten extra, and I also like to keep the ones I'm currently training for roping inside so I don't spend time I don't have chasing them down to saddle them. They need fed every morning, and the stalls all need cleaned out on a regular basis. We let them out in the second pasture from time to time, but some of them don't get along." He went through which horses didn't play well with others, and how the stallions obviously needed to be kept separate from the mares.

"This afternoon, we're teaching the kids to ride," he said, stopping in front of Chevy's stall to double-check she had enough feed. "It's supposed to be a break for them, but it means going over how to put on the saddle and bridle, and most of them don't know anything about horses—like not standing behind them or how to steer—and there's always someone who thinks they've got it down and goes too fast, so we've gotta keep an eye on them at all times."

"Whatever you need me to do, I'll do it." Sadie climbed onto the fence in front of Chevy. Royce was about to warn her that ever since she'd gotten pregnant, she was picky about who got close to her—pretty much him and him alone.

But when Sadie ran her hand down Chevy's neck, murmuring a hello, the horse nuzzled her like she was her long-lost best friend. Come to think of it, they were. Sadie had spent lots of time talking to Chevy before and after they loaded or unloaded for rodeos, and she'd ridden her a few times. And when Chevy had gotten a nasty cut on her leg after being caught up in a fence, Sadie was the one who'd kept her calm while he'd doctored the leg and administered the antibiotics.

She glanced at the horse's stomach. "You got yourself knocked up, girl?"

"Actually, it takes two to tango, in case you haven't

heard."

Sadie laughed, the happy noise filling the air. "Horse tango. Sounds like quite the show."

The other day, he'd thought he wanted to hear her laugh again, but now that it was echoing in his chest, reminding him how much he used to crave the sound, he was thinking it was just as dangerous as her licking her lips. He switched his focus back to his horse. "Casanova's the sire, actually—not that I watched the show. She was pasture bred."

Sadie's face brightened. "I'm glad you went with Casanova. I'm worried about him now that he's getting older, and it makes me sad to think of not having any other horses like him." She patted Chevy's side, and the horse nickered. "It still cracks me up that you named her Chevy."

"She's my ride. It fit." Since she obviously had no problem with Sadie, he saw an opportunity to give the pregnant mare the extra attention he wanted to give but simply didn't have time for. "She hasn't been brushed down well in a while, and I feel like I'm neglecting her, so if you find a few extra minutes to do that, I'd appreciate it."

"Sure. I'll take good care of her. Along with the rest of them." She jumped to the ground and looked up and down the line of stalls. Royce waited for her to complain about how dirty they were. She didn't, though, just headed to the wall with the tools and grabbed a pitchfork. He had to admit it was nice she knew so much about the ranch already—well, he'd admit it in his head, anyway.

"I'll send in help. Mom's divvying up assignments now. She's got all these rules she can go over more with you later, but the one you'll probably enforce most is the swear jar. It's a dollar every time they swear. Other than that, just keep them working. You've got to be firm, so they don't walk over you, but not so harsh they never want to talk to you again." He doubted she could be strict enough. He'd have Cory work nearby to keep an eye on her while she was getting the hang of everything.

"I'll keep that in mind." Sadie scooped up a big pile of crap and placed it in the wheelbarrow. Royce turned to leave, but then she said, "You know, when I quit my last job, I told my boss I'd rather shovel horseshit than work for him."

He slowly twisted back to her. "You did not."

"I was about to sign a recording contract, and the guy was a huge jerk, so I thought I'd leave with one of those *screw-you* speeches everyone dreams of giving but usually keeps in. So once the contract fell though, I knew I wasn't going back to that job. I wasn't lying, though." She scooped up another clump. "As crappy as this is—pun intended—I'd still choose it over those damn phone surveys."

She propped the pitchfork on the ground and looked across the barn at him. Pieces of her hair were slipping out of her ponytail, framing her face. Something deep inside of him twisted. "Thanks for the job, Royce. Seriously. I know I don't deserve you to be nice to me, and I know you didn't give me the job because you think I won't make it. I appreciate it."

Damn, damn, damn. He wanted to stay mad at her—to hold on to how badly the girl had hurt him when she'd left him the way she had. But years had passed, and here she was, thanking him for the opportunity to shovel shit. They were different people now, and maybe he really should give her a chance. Their romantic relationship was over, but maybe they could pull off being sort of friends. After all, she used to be the person he told all his secrets, hopes, and dreams to.

"You're welcome. But you might not be thanking me by the end of the day. Or when you see your wimpy paycheck." He shot her a quick smile and headed outside.

By the time he got over to the cabins, Mom already had everyone gathered and was doling out assignments.

"Actually," Royce cut in, "I want Eli, Addison, and Mark to go muck the stalls."

Addison's parents had caught her smoking weed and sent her here. She was a little spoiled but easygoing, and he had a bit of a soft spot for her, mostly because she was also funny. Not soft enough to keep her from the crappy chores, though—her parents wanted her "scared straight."

She wrinkled her nose. "Does muck mean—"

"Cleaning up horse crap. Yep."

"Great," Eli muttered, shaking his head.

Mom glanced at Royce, probably wondering if he was picking on Eli. For once, he wasn't using mucking the stalls as a punishment. He thought working with Sadie would be good for Eli, regardless of the job. "Just get going. Cory, can you make sure they get there straightaway? Ask Sadie to teach 'em more about the horses as they clean."

"Sadie?" Eli said, glancing toward the barn. It was tiny, but there was a hint of a smile. "She works here?"

"Just started today. Now go get to work, and don't give her any trouble. I've got an endless supply of hard jobs I can find for you if I need to."

The eye roll was back, but the kid picked up his step and headed toward the barn, ahead of the other two in his group instead of dragging behind. Everyone dispersed, leaving him and Mom.

"So...Sadie's working here now?" Mom asked.

Royce kicked at a rock jabbing out of the ground, breaking it free so he could scoot it off to the side with his boot before it became a tripping hazard. "You saw how good she was with Eli yesterday. And she's good with the animals—hell, she knows most of the horses, not to mention the land, and she can even drive a tractor if need be."

Mom raised an eyebrow. "Mm-hmm."

"Don't start psychoanalyzing me, Mom. She's qualified and desperate for a job I'm desperate to fill. That's it."

"Well, that's a very mature decision. I'm proud of you." She leaned in and kissed his cheek, then headed after the group that was going to be learning to milk the cows.

Now he was the one rolling his eyes. His mom probably already had him and Sadie back together in her mind. He hated to break it to her, but that was about as unlikely as his becoming the bronc-riding world champion.

• • •

"This is disgusting," Addison said, pulling up her shirt so that it covered her nose and mouth. "In fact, this is *torture*. I can deal with the other podunk stuff—it's even kind of fun, actually—but this? This is total bullshit!"

Sadie stuck her pitchfork in the ground and used it to prop herself up. "Okay, now you owe money to the swear jar." She didn't mind enforcing rules with the princess—the girl had done nothing but complain.

"It's not swearing if it's a noun instead of an expletive, and I'm referring to the stuff we have to pick up."

"It's actually horse crap, not bull crap, so that's not going to fly. I'm marking it down."

"Fine." Addison turned around, and Sadie was pretty sure she just got called a female dog, and not in the noun sense.

How did everyone here deal with the diva attitude? Eli put on a front, but the kid was funny, and he'd done twice as much as everyone else, including herself. She couldn't keep up. Her arms burned and, okay, it smelled awful, that sweet scent of hay mixing with the not so sweet. But at least they were almost done. She needed a break and about a gallon of water.

"As I was saying," Sadie said, taking up her spiel on the horses, "Chevy's a bay quarter horse. She's good for roping because of her muscular build that's great for quick bursts of energy, and she's gotta be strong when the cowboy ropes a calf or steer. Bay refers to her color, which is the reddish-brown coat and dark mane and tail. Since her baby daddy is a black quarter horse, it'll be interesting to see what her foal looks like."

"Baby daddy," Eli said with a chuckle.

"I know the baby daddy, too. He's my grandpa's horse." Sadie couldn't help adding a pun, since Eli had liked *baby daddy* so well. "Total stud."

Addison leaned against the handle of her pitchfork, scowl firmly in place. "Isn't the baby called a colt?"

"Only if it's a boy. I should've asked Royce if he knew girl or boy." Now that she thought about it, she doubted he'd spend money on finding out. "If it's a girl, it's a filly."

"How do you know Royce anyway?" Addison asked. "Yesterday you guys looked like you could barely stand each other, and now you're working here."

Okay, this chick was getting on Sadie's last nerve. "We went to high school together. Now, help Mark take the wheelbarrow out of the barn."

Mark had hardly said a word, just worked now and then and looked from person to person, like he was soaking it all in but choosing not to comment. He took hold of the wheelbarrow, and Addison took a handle, more for show, because she clearly wasn't helping much.

"That girl is—" Sadie cut herself off, realizing she shouldn't bad-mouth her, especially not to Eli.

The hint of a dimple showed up in Eli's cheek when a smile crossed his lips. "She thinks she's pretty tough, but she's mostly talk. I thought she was hot at first."

"Not anymore?"

"Well, yeah, she's still hot, but she's…" He shook his head. "Complicated. I think her last boyfriend messed her up, because she's like, anti-guy, and everyone's an assho—Jerk."

A tiny bit of sympathy for the girl crept in. Sadie had dated a couple of jerks—enough to understand how they could make it seem not worth trying again. Even though it was one of the hardest decisions she'd ever made, she'd turned down Royce's proposal because she'd wanted to follow her singing dream, and she was trying to keep her priorities straight, the way she'd always promised herself she would. But admittedly, she hadn't realized what she'd had when she dated him. She'd had no idea how many guys out there only called when they wanted sex, never thought of anyone but themselves, and cheated on girls because they could—luckily she'd learned that lesson secondhand, through one of her roommates in Nashville.

Sadie's best relationship—probably the best she'd ever have—was definitely all those years ago, and she'd taken it for granted. She wasn't sure if it was incredibly unfair, or if she was incredibly lucky that she got to experience love like that at least once in her life.

Royce was obviously working to keep up a crabby exterior, but she knew the truth about the good guy underneath it. She thought about the brief moments when the softer Royce crept through, wondering if she could coax it out full-time if she tried.

"Plus we're only here for the first half of the summer," Eli said, pulling her out of her thoughts and effectively reminding her that it was only a matter time before she'd go back to Nashville. Getting close to Royce only to leave again wouldn't be fair to him or to her still-cracked heart.

She smiled at Eli, though, happy he'd put it that way, instead of implying he could just use Addison for that long. "You never know. If you like her, I say go for it. But only if you're going to prove to her that not all guys are jerks."

"That's another problem. I might prove the opposite."

Sadie studied him for a moment and then shook her head. "Not buying it. Secret's out—you're a nice guy."

"Yeah. That's how I ended up here."

It was almost like he wanted to tell her why he was there, but then Addison and Mark came in, and the moment was ruined.

Royce came in and inspected the stalls. They'd done the best they could, but Sadie held her breath, knowing it wasn't perfect and wondering if he'd tell her she didn't do a good enough job.

"Looks good." He finally turned to her. "Any problems?"

She glanced at Addison—not that she was such a problem, but Royce had said she needed to be strict. Was this when she brought up the swear jar? Addison's eyes widened.

Sadie slowly peeled off her gloves, letting the girl stew

for a moment. "Nope. No problems."

"Then time for lunch."

As Addison walked by, Sadie whispered, "I'll let the swearing slide this once. It won't happen again."

The girl's eyes narrowed—apparently, warning or not, the girl wasn't letting go of her bitterness—and then she followed after Eli and Mark.

Sadie picked up the horse brush.

"What are you doing?" Royce asked.

"We barely got done with the stalls, so I haven't had a chance to brush down Chevy yet."

"It can be done later. Come eat."

"It's okay. I'll just skip lunch." Sadie reached up with the brush, but then Royce was right by her, gently gripping her elbow. As minor as it was, the contact was still enough to make it hard for her to keep air moving in and out of her lungs. She could feel each one of his callused fingertips on her bare skin, radiating little spots of heat.

"You can't skip meals. Is that what you normally do? You're so scrawny I'm surprised you can even lift a pitchfork."

Her jaw dropped. She thought they had a truce—that they were going to stop baiting each other and be nice. Only his face made it seem like he didn't realize he was insulting her. There was almost... Was that concern in his eyes?

He let go of her arm and stepped back. "Just eat a cheeseburger or five, will you? Consider it part of the job." With that, he turned and left the barn, muttering to himself.

Sadie set the brush down and stared after him, her breaths coming out shakier than they had earlier, when she'd been doing manual labor.

Chapter Six

Sadie was getting used to her new life one day at a time, until two weeks of working at the ranch had passed. Her job included a lot of physical labor, but she loved working with the animals, and whenever she could, she'd ride a horse to the river so she could soak in the beauty of the rushing water and pine trees. Being there made her homesick almost, which was strange because she *was* home. Somehow she'd forgotten how many great things there were about Hope Springs, and lately she was seeing the place in a new light. Yes, it was small and there wasn't a mall for miles, but there were also long stretches of untamed land and a peace she'd never felt in the city.

Royce didn't talk to her much, only to give instructions here and there, and more often than not he sent Cory to tell her what needed to be done next. So she focused on the work, how nice it was to do something different every day and not be confined to an office, and the fact that she was employed and blessedly tired by the time she made it back home—at least then her lack of a social life didn't seem so depressing.

"Hey," Eli said as she brought Bud back inside the barn. "I was looking for you. Wanted to show you something."

As for the youth camp side of things, Addison still disliked her and didn't bother hiding it, but the rest of the kids were easy to get along with, and she was always glad on the days when she got to work with Eli.

He took the sketch pad out from under his arm and extended it to her. Sadie flipped through images of trees, horses, the river, and several of the other teens. There was one of Addison sitting on a tree stump, frowning at the moss-covered hook on the end of her fishing pole.

"Did that one yesterday, while everyone was fishing. She was so mad she didn't catch anything but moss," he said with a laugh.

Sadie had rolled her eyes at the girl's pouting, but Eli's drawing showed the humor in the situation, and guessing from the detail, he was still a bit intrigued with Addison's beauty. "They're amazing, Eli. You're a great artist."

He shot her a shy, crooked grin. "Thanks." He set his pad off to the side, took Bud from her, and started to undo the saddle. "I used to spend hours in my room with just my music, sketch pad, and pencils. Then my parents decided I wasn't 'engaged enough.'"

Eli slid the saddle off Bud and Sadie took off the bridle. Once in a while he'd make a comment about home, but they were usually around too many other people for him to divulge much about it. "We had fights over stupid stuff, too. Just normal crap like cleaning my room, and when I did want to go out, they wouldn't let me because my friends were"—Eli made air quotes—"'bad influences.'"

The kids' counseling sessions were private, but Caroline had given Sadie the basic rundown of the teens, so she'd know how to better handle situations as they arose. So she knew Eli's parents were concerned that he had anger issues and possibly a drug problem because of his mood swings. Caroline thought it was typical teenage stuff, surges of hormones and frustrations over no one understanding him.

"So they told me I had to go out for sports." Eli turned to face her and leaned back against one of the posts. "I'd played baseball in junior high and they wanted me to try out for the team. I did to get them off my back, suffered through practices I hated, and figured at least I could draw on the bus to away games. While the JV team was playing one night, I found a teammate picking on a guy from my art class. So I punched him."

Part of her wanted to give Eli a high five for standing up for his friend—she hated bullies. But she assumed encouraging physical violence wasn't the way to go.

"Anyway, I got suspended, and then my parents told me they were sending me here for the first part of summer. All because I joined the team like *they* wanted."

"And maybe a little tiny bit because of the punching?" Sadie asked, raising her eyebrows.

Eli rolled his eyes, but there was a hint of a smile playing across his lips. "I'm just saying that I never would've been there if they hadn't insisted I go out for baseball in the first place."

Sadie bumped her shoulder into his. "And then you wouldn't be here, and who would I talk to?"

"True. So if you think about it, I really punched the guy for you."

Sadie laughed. "Sure, just throw me under the bus. Way to take responsibility, dude." Seeing how he'd bonded with the horses and how easily smiles came these days made her appreciate even more what this place did for teens like Eli.

He grinned and picked up his sketch pad. "I gotta get back. I have to meet with Mrs. Dixon in five, and if I'm even a minute late, I'll get more chores."

"See you later." Sadie put Bud in his stall and made sure the gate was latched. While she liked working with the teens, she also enjoyed when she got a few peaceful moments alone with the horses.

She moved over to Chevy's stall. "It's been a hot day, and it's a bit dusty in here. I think you could use a bath. What do you think?"

Chevy neighed and nudged Sadie with her nose.

"That's what I think, too," Sadie replied, used to chatting and translating for the animals now. Just call her Dr. Doolittle. She unlatched the stall and led Chevy outside. Within a few minutes, she had the hose hooked up and the water turned on, the nozzle on the end allowing her to spray farther with a simple pull of the trigger. As she ran the water over Chevy, she started to hum "Before He Cheats."

When she got to the chorus, she went ahead and threw in a few dance moves as she belted out the lyrics—there was really no other way to sing Carrie. Water droplets rained down on her as she twirled, and Chevy pranced around like she wanted to get in on the singing and dancing, too.

"Hey."

The deep voice startled her so much that she dropped

the hose. When she spun around, Royce was standing behind her, sunlight glowing around him and casting his features in shadow. As he stepped closer, though, she could clearly make out his amused grin.

She'd nearly forgotten the impact of his full smile. The way it lit up his eyes, showed off his strong jawline, and made attraction thrum through her veins. She licked her suddenly dry lips. "Hey. I was just…" She picked up the hose and gestured to Chevy, who shook out her mane, sending water all over Sadie.

She shrieked, and Royce's low chuckle drifted toward her. He came over, and Chevy whinnied, moving her head toward him. Even though there was still lots of space between her and Royce, Sadie's pulse skittered. It should be getting easier to be around him, but her body hadn't seemed to figure that out yet.

He ran his hand down the horse's damp neck. "So, how's she doing?"

"Seems good," Sadie said. "She's eating and her energy's up—I walked her around the corral a couple of times this morning. She's getting pretty big, though."

One corner of Royce's mouth kicked up. "I was actually asking her about you."

"Well, clearly she thinks I'm awesome."

He was fighting it, but the other side of his mouth was trying to take the half smile to a full one—two in one day. A record! "And she likes the singing, too, I'd bet."

"She doesn't complain, anyway. As you saw, sometimes she even joins in."

Royce looked down at her, the brim of his hat making it hard to get a good read on his expression. He opened his mouth, then closed it and shook his head.

"What?"

"Nothing. I'll leave you to it." He patted Chevy's neck and then started away, same as he'd been doing for the past two weeks. That was the most they'd talked about anything not job related, and since his horse was involved, Sadie wasn't even sure she could say that.

She'd missed him for six years, but in a distant, once-in-a-while way. But being next to him, remembering how much they used to talk and laugh, in addition to all the kisses and intimate moments, and still having so much distance between them?

It made her heart feel like someone had turned it inside out.

Defeated, she lifted the nozzle, circling around the front of Chevy to finish giving her a bath. She glanced at Royce's retreating figure, and she wasn't sure what exactly got into her, but suddenly she found herself turning the nozzle toward him. She aimed right at his back and pulled the trigger.

His spine went stick straight, and then he slowly spun around. Her heart sped and she gripped the nozzle tighter, not sure whether to break into laughter or run. "Sadie…" he said, his voice dangerously low.

"Yes?" she replied in her most innocent tone. Then she went ahead and pulled the trigger again, hitting him square in the chest.

He charged, and she squealed, nearly tripping backward over her feet as he rushed toward her. He ate up the distance in a couple of long strides, and as she fought for control of the hose, she was thinking that running would've been the right move. Trying to curl herself around the nozzle to keep it out of his hands was no use—Royce was too strong. He pried it from her fingers, pointed it at her, and pulled the trigger. Water pelted her in the chest, and she gasped as it ran down her shirt.

"Not so smug now, are we?" Royce said with a chuckle, his finger curling around the trigger again. She held up her hands and took a step back, but instead of taking it as a surrender move, he apparently took it as a sign to let loose the spray again.

"Royce!"

"Yes?" he said, mimicking her from earlier, while flicking his wrist to make sure the water got her from head to toe. She laughed and swatted the stream back at him, which was mostly ineffective, but at least got him a little wet. Through the sparkling droplets, she saw a victorious grin curve his lips— Oh, he thought he'd won, did he?

She dove for the nozzle, grasping it in a death grip. Water continued to spray everywhere as she tried to twist it back to face him. Chevy circled them, nudging them with her nose, until all three of them were dripping wet.

That was when Sadie noticed that they'd gathered quite the audience. The teens and Caroline were all staring, jaws slack. Royce's grip on her and the hose loosened, and he was starting to get that stern, too-serious expression. Worried this was about to turn into a big deal and ruin the happy vibe she'd finally managed to get with him, she grabbed the nozzle from Royce and sprayed Eli.

He didn't miss a beat. He grabbed a bucket, scooped water up from the nearby trough, and tossed it at her. Excited shouts and squeals went up as the water flew and more people jumped in. Before long, every single member of the camp was involved. Alliances formed, the ground became slick with mud, and laughter filled the air.

After everyone was beyond soaked, Caroline called the fight, telling everyone to go change and then meet at the barn in twenty for afternoon chores. Sadie reached for Chevy's bridle to lead her back into the stalls—that was probably more than enough excitement for a pregnant horse in one day.

Royce stepped in front of her, quite the sight now that his hair was dripping wet and his clothes were plastered to his skin. "So, tonight we're gonna build a big fire and have hot dogs and s'mores. It's a reward for the kids, since they've worked so hard. Thought you might want to be there." He wiped at the dirt that'd gotten on his hat when it'd fallen off in the scuffle. "Unless you've got other plans?"

"Oh. No. I mean, no other plans. I'll just go home and change, and then come back?"

"Good." Royce nodded. Then he was off, and she was standing there, fighting the urge to break into another song and dance.

• • •

Royce stared at the cloudless evening sky. It wouldn't be long before the sun was completely gone from the day and the sky was inky black. Growing up, he used to gaze at the stars, listen to the silence, and feel like the only person in the world. Then his parents had started the Alternative Ranch Camp for Youth, the two extra cabins were built, and he'd have to drive or ride out a couple of miles to feel alone. All he'd ever wanted to be was a cowboy. Yes, there were the rodeo competitions, and he'd thought he'd do them longer, but ranching had always been his long-term goal. He wasn't sure he was very good at running the camp, but he was trying his best, and he had his land and his horses and he was happy with just that.

Until Sadie came back, and he'd gone and started missing the way they used to talk. Her smile, the sound of her laugh. The way she challenged him and drove him crazy in every possible way—she was free in a way most people never were. Like with those dance moves and the water fight, turning work into her very own party.

Back in high school, they'd drive a few miles from the house and lie in the back of his truck to look at stars. Anyway, that was his pretense for getting her out there. Stargazing was nice and all, but really it was more a chance to be alone with her than talk constellations. And man, had they taken advantage of all that alone time, all those nights under the clear sky. When it was too cold, they'd maneuver around in the cab of his truck, taking it as a fun challenge instead of a hitch in their plans.

Desire wound through him, heating his blood. His body remembered her too well, all the ways they used to be perfect for each other. But it hadn't been enough for her. She'd talked about pursuing a singing career, and he'd always admired her ambition, but he'd thought she could do it from here. With him. He would've supported her. Which just proved he'd had no idea what it really took to become a famous singer.

He probably shouldn't have proposed that summer, but he'd loved her, and he could feel her slipping away. He'd thought it'd tie them together instead of tear them apart forever.

This is stupid. I can't keep thinking about the past. Inviting her tonight was stupid, too, but she worked hard, and the nights around the fire were a reward for all of them. It was unfair for her to miss out because he couldn't get his head straight.

He'd thought he'd been doing a pretty good job until this afternoon. Now all he could think about was her laughing and squealing as the water rained down on them, her wet T-shirt clinging to every curve of her skin. He wasn't sure he'd ever get that image out of his mind.

I should've never let it get that far.

That's it. Cory and I gotta get out more. I need to be around women who aren't Sadie. Maybe he'd even remind himself how easy picking one up could be. Then he'd get this stir-crazy feeling out of his system and be able to focus again.

The fire wasn't started yet, and Sadie was in short sleeves, standing next to the pit and rubbing her arms. Even with the fire, the temperature at night usually dropped enough to need a coat. Not to mention Sadie had always run colder than he did, and even with his long-sleeved flannel and light jacket on, he was still plenty cool.

What's she doing running around without a jacket?

She shivered, hugging her arms tighter around her. Maybe if she had an ounce of body fat, she wouldn't be on the verge of hypothermia.

"Mark, Eli, and Brady, go get some wood. Addison, grab the matches from Mrs. Dixon, will you?" Royce shook off his jacket and tossed it at Sadie. It hit her in the face before she caught it in her arms. *Oops.*

Her mouth dropped open, and he was sure he was about

to get it, but then she just slipped into the too-big jacket. Her big green eyes were on him, and he was starting to feel that desire again, twisting at his gut, making him want to reach out and wrap his arms around her so she'd be even warmer.

He clenched his jaw, hating that she cut so easily through the defenses he'd worked to build. "Did you forget how to make a fire? You could've gotten to work on that instead of jumping around to keep yourself warm."

"I thought maybe it was part of your teaching experience and I didn't want to mess it up. But here, take your damn coat back and I'll build the stupid-ass fire," she said, starting to undo the zipper she'd just finished closing.

"You owe money to the swear jar," Addison said as she approached.

Royce took a large step forward and put his hands on Sadie's shoulders to keep her from pulling her arms out of the sleeves. "I'm sorry, okay? Just keep the jacket on." He didn't know why he got so irritated every time he started feeling soft toward her. Maybe it was his defense mechanism kicking in, but he was struggling to find the right balance, too far to the friendly side one minute, and then way too far the other the next. He needed to get it better under control before he ruined the progress they'd made.

He tilted his head toward Addison. "She is right about the swear jar, though—two in one sentence, even. That's a pretty heavy fine. Why don't you help me get the branches for roasting and we'll consider you paid up."

Sadie narrowed her eyes at him, then she tugged the jacket closed and marched toward the bushes where it was easiest to find good hot-dog-roasting sticks.

He scratched the back of his neck, trying to come up

with something to smooth it over. "So, what do you think about the program now that you've been around it for a couple weeks?"

"I don't know what I expected, but I'm surprised. I mean, there's only one of them who gets under my skin, and you guys give them more work than I expected, yet more freedom, too, if that makes sense."

"It's a work/reward system that my mom and dad perfected over the years. Like tonight we'll give them all knives so they can carve their own sticks. We could easily buy those fancy metal ones—my mom has some, in fact. But this way, it keeps them busy and shows them they've earned our trust. Over all the years, we've only had a handful of kids who were on a weapons ban, where they couldn't be trusted with anything like a pitchfork, shovel, or tiny pocketknife." He stepped over a large rock. "Which one gets under your skin? Eli?" She sure hid it well, and he was a little disappointed. He thought they'd sort of bonded.

"No, Eli's awesome! That kid's going to be a famous artist someday, mark my words. That Addison chick hates me, and I"—she lowered her voice—"I find it hard to like her. Guess that means I fail at working the camp side of things."

"Are you kidding me? All of us have had kids we can't stand, even my mom, although she's the best at hiding it. I was having so much trouble with Eli, but he's changed since you started working here." Royce noticed that she expected him to be famous—that was the only way success was achieved with her, apparently. "Addison's got a big attitude, but she's funny, and she really pulls the rest of them together."

"I guess that's why it's good to have several people

working with them. Everyone connects to someone different and even to different aspects of the work. I love that it's part of my job description to take the time to talk with and listen to someone who needs it, by the way—every other job I've had, my chattiness has gotten me into trouble. I hate rules for when people are allowed to talk and for how long."

Oh, he remembered, and he couldn't help smiling. Chattiness was an understatement—it was more like she was compelled to talk. Back in high school, she and Quinn were constantly assigned to sit far apart in classes because they couldn't be quiet when they were together, and long road trips to rodeos had been filled with discussions about whatever topic popped into her head.

A cool breeze floated over them, swirling strands of Sadie's hair around her face. "What I'm saying is, it's a good thing, what you're doing here. I saw it when I came over back in high school, of course, I just didn't realize how intensive and challenging it was."

Yeah, she knew how to talk, but she also knew how to genuinely listen. So he said the thing he constantly thought but always held in. "I'm not as good at it as my dad was. And no matter how hard I try, I never will be. I'm just trying not to completely screw up his legacy."

Sadie stopped and turned to face him. "You're good at it, Royce. Way better than you give yourself credit for." She reached out and squeezed his arm. His eyes met hers and he swallowed, too aware of the freckles across the bridge of her nose and the way his skin hummed under her touch. "You're *not* screwing it up. In fact, to put it in cowboy terms the way your dad or my grandpa would"—she cleared her throat—"you're doin' a damn fine job." He assumed the low, half-growly way she said it was her impression of a dude. Who knew that a mock guy voice could sound so cute? She smirked, one eyebrow arching higher than the other. "Take that, swear jar!"

"Thanks," he said with a smile, and the dull ache that'd risen up faded away. He hadn't realized how badly he needed to hear that.

She dropped her hand, and his arm suddenly felt cold and empty.

Focus, Dixon. Don't even think about kissing her. He couldn't stop staring at her lips now, though. Remembering the way she used to sigh when he kissed her. He quickly stepped past her, glad they were so close to the bushes.

"I've got an extra knife you can—"

"Give me some credit," she said, pulling out a pocketknife and grabbing a branch. "I'm at least half prepared for tonight." For a little while, they gathered sticks in silence. And whenever she turned around or bent over, he took advantage of the opportunity to check out her butt.

Like he said before, old habits died hard.

• • •

Sadie glanced at Royce's backside as she followed him to the now-glowing fire, a bundle of sticks in her hand. Earlier, when he'd thrown the coat in her face, he'd seemed mad at her, his expression and gruff words at odds with the fact that he'd noticed she was cold. While she was grateful for the warmth, she wasn't going to just let him be a jerk to her. But when she'd been about to throw the coat back at him and stomp away, he'd softened again. Then things were easy, the way they used to be, and she swore they'd almost had a moment. She wasn't sure if it was an I-don't-completely-hate-you moment or something more.

A glimmer of hope rose up. Maybe they could be friends. After all, she wasn't sure how long she was going to stay in Hope Springs, and she could really use a friend as she figured out her messy life and got a game plan for the next step to get it back on the right track.

Royce handed out the sticks to the kids, and she did the same with the ones she'd gathered. When they met in the middle, he actually smiled at her. *Friends who kiss might be good.*

"Everyone grab a knife and get the end sharpened so you can cook your hot dog. And yes, Addison," Royce said, glancing at the girl, "I remembered your veggie dogs, even though I had to drive to the next town over to get them."

The girl beamed at him, and Sadie was sure her expression matched. How could Royce think he wasn't good at this? She settled on a log next to Cory, who was in a foldout chair, sliding a hot dog onto the end of an already sharpened stick.

"How often do you guys do this?" she asked.

"We usually work the kids pretty hard for the first three weeks. That seems to be the perfect amount of time for them to know what we expect and to learn most of what they need to know. Then we find we can ease back a little without losing control. If they work hard all week, we have these on Friday nights, and give them Saturday and Sunday off, all except for cooking. If one of them gets feisty or troublesome, they work while everyone else plays. It's good motivation."

Sadie started carving the end of her stick, watching

the pale wood shavings curl away and drift to the ground, while the scent of smoke and meat filled the air. "I'm glad Royce has you to help him out." She bit her lip, thinking she shouldn't meddle, but since when did that stop her? "He puts on a tough front, but how's he really doing with running everything by himself and dealing with his dad's death?"

Cory glanced sideways at her. "Sadie, I've always liked you, and we're still cool. But I'm not gettin' in the middle of you two. You want to know, you ask him."

"You know he won't tell me." He'd hinted at struggling with the camp when they'd been gathering branches, but he'd shut it down pretty quickly, walking off before she could dig any deeper. "Can't I worry about a friend?"

One of Cory's eyebrows arched, disappearing under the brim of his hat. "A friend?"

Sadie's shoulders sagged. "Fine. A work colleague."

"We both know it's more than either of those things. He's doing okay, and that's all I'm sayin'. I'm not a chick and this ain't no damn slumber party."

Sadie rolled her eyes but couldn't help but smile. What was it with guys and their inability to admit that they actually had emotions?

Royce came over and sat next to her on the log. She'd assumed he would go back to keeping his distance the rest of the night. Now here he was, sitting so close she could reach out and touch him. She became acutely aware of his knee resting against hers, and how he smelled like woods and hay and a hint of campfire. She watched the firelight dance on the planes of his face. He pushed up his sleeves, and then her attention was on the way the muscles in his forearms moved as he whittled the end of his branch into a point.

When he finished, he handed her a hot dog. She slid it onto her stick and leaned forward, putting the end over the flames. Everyone all around them was doing the same thing, multiple conversations going on.

The log rocked as Royce leaned forward. Sadie wobbled and his arm came around her waist. "Careful," he said, his lips so close to her ear that goose bumps broke out across her skin. Then she turned her head and looked into his brown, brown eyes.

He dropped his arm and moved his focus to his roasting hot dog. Then he turned to Cory and they started talking about whether or not the hay in the back field was ready to rake. It was like high school, only she, Royce, and Cory would've been around a bonfire somewhere else, drinking cheap beer and discussing the last or next rodeo.

And Royce's hand would be clamped onto her thigh, and she'd have her head on his shoulder.

"Now what do we do?" Addison asked.

"Eat more. Relax. Look at the stars. Take your pick." Royce glanced at Cory. "Once Cory here's done eating, he'll pull out the guitar."

"And maybe Sadie can sing for us," Cory said.

Sadie almost choked on her food. She swallowed the bite in her mouth and said, "No thanks." The memory of the last time she was onstage played through her mind. Earlier that afternoon, she'd learned her recording dreams had fallen through once again, and while she'd wanted to cancel the gig, she told herself the show must go on. But then she'd gone to sing a song she'd sung countless times, only for her voice to crack. She'd struggled to fix it but missed the next few notes as well. Every doubt she'd ever had rose up as sorrow and the overwhelming sense of rejection clawed at her, and then she'd done something she'd sworn she'd never do: she left the stage midsong. By the time she'd gotten into her car and driven away, the tears were pouring down her face.

"I wanna hear you sing," Eli said, leaning forward.

She shot him a *shut-it* look. He was supposed to be on her side.

"I showed you my art. I think it's only fair."

Someone started chanting, "Sing, sing," and it caught on like wildfire. Cory shoved the remaining half of his hot dog in his mouth, got out of his seat, and reappeared with his guitar a minute or so later.

Panic rose up, sharp enough it stung her lungs. Singing to a crowd of jaded teens who probably hated country music hardly seemed like a good way to get her confidence back. Eli raised his voice over the chanting. "What, you too cool for this stuff?" he asked, echoing the words she'd said to him the first day they met.

I'm stuck now, she thought, slowly standing so her diaphragm wouldn't be all squished up and she'd have a better shot at getting the best sound possible. "Okay. One song."

It's just a small group. No mic, no crowd expecting a brilliant performance.

Along with the apprehension clenching Sadie's stomach, a tingle of excitement mixed in. Somewhere along the way, singing had become a source of stress. Out here, just her and Cory's guitar—well, it was the type of singing she loved.

With her panic easing the tiniest bit, she was at least able to get a little air back in her lungs.

Cory played a couple chords. "Let me guess, you want me to play 'Honky Tonk Badonkadonk.'"

Sadie shot Cory a dirty look and his grin widened. Like she'd really want to sing an offensive song about girls' butts. "Funny," she said, and despite her nerves, she found herself smiling. "But *so* not gonna happen."

Cory laughed and so did Royce—that helped, too. It was almost like old times all over again.

"How about 'Before He Cheats' and I act out the music video using your truck?" She made a big show of looking around. "Where's a baseball bat?"

"Hey, do you guys know any Lady Antebellum?" Addison asked, and Sadie whipped her head toward the girl, surprised she knew any country groups, even though that one was pretty crossover. "I actually kind of like them."

Sadie glanced at Cory. He nodded and started playing the intro to "Just a Kiss."

Her heart was pounding fast, which was pretty inconvenient considering it had relocated to her throat. She blew out her breath and closed her eyes for a moment, centering herself with the music… Then she started, quieter than she usually did, but the notes were right. Cory sang softly along with her, taking the guy's part, and while he always rebuffed the compliment, he did have a good voice. With each word, she put more behind it until instinct took over and she was belting out the lyrics, the way she used to when it was all about the music. By the second verse, she got up the courage to look at some of the faces.

And when she was singing about shots in the dark and just a kiss good night, how could she not sing at Royce? She didn't want to mess everything up, but she found herself hoping that maybe someday she'd get to kiss him again—because the thought of not being able to made a tight band form around her chest.

Then the song was over and adrenaline was pumping through her veins, giving her that floaty performing buzz. There really was nothing else like it. *I did it!*

The little group applauded. Addison even said, "Wow, that was really good!" Maybe Royce was right—she should give the girl a chance. Sadie gave a little bow, settled back on the log next to Royce, and stole a peek at him.

He shot up, rubbing his palms on his jeans. "Looks like we're out of drinks. I'll be right back." He took large strides toward the house, fading into the blackness.

For weeks, things had been stilted between her and Royce, but today it felt like the barriers were coming down, and the song had her thinking about taking chances before they slipped away. "I'm just going to see if he needs help."

Sadie had underestimated the walk back—not the distance, but she kept wobbling on the uneven ground and tripping across rocks she didn't see. Royce's place was dark, a black outline against a sky almost as black.

If I fall and break something, he'll probably scold me for not having a flashlight. Not like *he* was using one. The lights in his house snapped on, sending enough of a glow for her to see by. Her booted footsteps on the wooden steps sounded loud in the silence.

She almost smacked into him as he came out balancing a couple of six-packs of Coke in his arms. "Whoa, sorry. I thought you might need some help." Her words came out all together, one big blur she hoped made sense.

His eyebrows lowered. "With soda?"

"Well…yeah? I guess?" *Great, now I'm talking in all questions.*

"I got it."

She scratched the side of her forehead, which had suddenly become uncontrollably itchy. Now that she was face-to-face with him, she was rethinking everything, unsure what she'd been doing following after him. As if things would magically be all good between them because of a water fight, a conversation about Second Chance Ranch, and one song around a campfire. "I guess I'll just…" She gestured at the fire burning in the distance. She headed down the stairs, holding the rail so she wouldn't fall and turn this moment from awkward to embarrassing.

"Sadie."

She spun around, and Royce came down a step, still one above her. "About what I said that first night in the grocery store about you not being on the radio…I should've never said it. For what it's worth, I always thought you'd make it. And when you sang tonight?" His dark eyes locked onto hers. "Well, it blows my mind that you didn't."

Sadie ran her hand up and down the polished wood railing, her heart expanding at his words. But then she remembered all those years ago, when she'd told him what she wanted to do and he hadn't said a word, simply stared at her like she was speaking another language. "Why didn't you tell me that before I left?" *I desperately needed to hear that all those years ago.*

"Why do you think?" He took another step down, but because of his height and the uneven ground she was standing on, he was still looming over her enough that she had to crane her neck. His fingers trailed down her arm, and even with the layers of fabric between them, she felt his touch in her core. "I was in love with you, and I thought that was enough. I thought I could make you happy."

"Royce."

He squeezed her hand once, firm and quick, and then continued toward the campfire. If he thought he could say something like that and just walk away, he had another thing coming.

• • •

Damn it, why had he admitted all that? It must've been the singing—he remembered learning about sirens in school, how they'd sing and make men lose their minds. He'd thought it was stupid, but now he got it.

"Royce, slow down." Sadie caught up to him, but he didn't dare look at her. She grabbed onto his elbow and he reluctantly stopped.

"You can't just walk away."

"Why? Because that's your thing?"

"That's not fair. You know I loved you, too. You think it was easy making that choice?"

He stared over at the flickering flames of the fire. "Look, I'm over it—glad, actually, that things worked out the way they did. All I was trying to say was that you should've made it. Let's not make a big deal of it."

"But it *is* a big deal. I had to try." Sadie stepped in front of him. Her eyes shone in a way that let him know she was holding back tears. "I knew I'd always wonder. Always regret not giving the singing thing my best shot. In the end, it would've driven us apart."

He shook his head, tamping down the flood of emotions trying to rise up in him. "I'm not doing this, Sadie. The past is the past."

"I just…" She shrugged. "I miss you." There was no denying he'd missed her, too, but he couldn't say it. Couldn't let himself go there again.

She put her hand on his arm and stepped so close her chest pressed against his. The moonlight glowed on her hair, highlighted her pretty features and spotlighted her full lips. He wanted to drop the soda, take her in his arms, and kiss her. Desire seared a path through his veins and his heart started pumping faster and faster. He shouldn't still want her the way he did, but heaven help him, he did. Every inch of him trembled with want.

It'd be too easy to pretend he could give in to it without consequence, but having Sadie as an employee helped minimize risks. Things were finally getting manageable, and he needed her to stay working at the ranch as long as possible. After the whole mess with Cory's girlfriend quitting after he broke up with her, Royce knew better than to try to mix business and relationships—especially knowing how volatile he and Sadie were together. The odds of it not affecting the camp were pretty much zero, and he couldn't afford to screw up what was keeping his land and Mom's alternative camp protected.

No, he had to be smart, something he rarely was when it came to Sadie. "The ranch and the camp are my life, and my responsibility is to them. I won't do anything to mess that up. You and I work together, and I have enough on my plate to deal with without adding complications. We need to keep things on a professional level. Do you understand?"

Her chin quivered, and he had to clench every muscle in his body to keep from reaching out to console her. It was so unfair how girls could cry and make you feel like shit.

"I understand." Her eyes lit on his and his stomach lurched. "But if you want to keep things professional, that also means not being an ass to me. I know it's not all the time, but I don't deserve it."

"You're right. I'm sorry. You being here has helped me a ton. I should've told you that sooner."

"Thanks." She reached up and wrapped a strand of hair around her finger. "Maybe we could even be friends? I could really use a friend right now."

His insides turned to mush. "Well, you've got me. But that's all it can be." The words came out thick, hitting him harder than he'd thought they would. He immediately wanted to take them back, but he held on to his resolve, telling himself it was for the best for both of them in the long run.

Her smile was laced with sadness, but at least it was a smile. She hooked her hand in the crook of her elbow and they headed toward the rest of their group.

Maybe they really could be friends. But already, he was starting to feel like he was getting lost in her.

Chapter Seven

The friendship with Royce was coming along better than expected. Lately they'd gotten along and had conversations that lasted almost a full ten minutes. Of course he'd chosen now to get ready for the upcoming Fourth of July rodeo, what with it being a month away, and watching him rope and ride was a new form of torture. But Sadie had only wanted to throw herself at him a couple of times. A day. Or maybe more like a couple times an hour, if she were being completely honest. So, yeah…totally friends.

It was progress, anyway.

Still, when her best friend let her know that she was coming to town for a visit, Sadie called an emergency meeting at the Dairy Freeze. At the time she'd been focused on the getting-ice-cream aspect, but as soon as she stepped inside, she knew she should've chosen another location. The Dairy Freeze was just another one of those frozen-in-time places, bursting at the seams with memories of being here with Royce after school, sitting on his lap as they shared the five-scoop banana split.

There were also framed newspaper clippings covering the wall, everything from town awards to school sporting events. Sadie's attention was drawn to the one in the middle. Mr. Hamilton, who owned the place, had sponsored Royce for the rodeo in Casper that went on during the state fair. She and Royce had driven down to stay with her dad, and Sadie had chewed her fingernails to the nubs—not only because she was singing three songs onstage to warm up the crowd at the fair, but also because she was nervous for Royce. Roping was one thing, but she hated the bronc riding, and bigger rodeos always meant rougher horses. Every time she watched him ride those bucking broncos, each second stretched into an eternity, and she'd sit there imagining every gory scenario involving her boyfriend getting kicked or stomped on.

And now the town's talked him into riding again for the local rodeo, even though he hasn't done it for years.

Sadie frowned at the article detailing Royce's All-Around Cowboy title thanks to winning all three of his events, her heart tugging as the bittersweet memories and regret slammed into her for about the kajillionth time since she'd moved back into town. *Isn't it about time they update the wall? Surely someone's done something newsworthy since then.*

"Sadie Hart, is that really you?"

She spun to face Quinn and squealed—she couldn't help it. A couple quick strides and they were hugging. Quinn had headed to the University of Wyoming in Cheyenne shortly after Sadie had taken off for Nashville. Now she was a bigwig at the Sakatas' real-estate development office there, which was funny because she'd always sworn she *absolutely wasn't* going into the family business. The Sakatas owned and managed half the commercial real estate in Wyoming, as well as northern Colorado and Utah. Hope Springs was a central location between all of their offices, so they'd built a summer house here and ended up staying full-time while Quinn and her sister attended school.

"I'm so excited we managed to be in town at the same time," Quinn said.

"Me, too." Sadie pulled back and studied her best friend—they'd texted and emailed, but it'd been years since they'd managed a meet up. Quinn still did the cat-eye thing with her black eyeliner that accented her exotic eyes—she used to joke that she was going to be the first famous Asian cowgirl, even though her only cowgirl experience was living in a tiny town and occasionally riding a horse.

Then they'd found out "Asian cowgirl" was a slang term for a sex position and had to stop using it—that was a whole different level of aspiration.

Sadie lifted a strand of Quinn's shiny, perfectly straight dark hair. "Look at you, all business." Back in high school she was forever putting red, blue, or purple streaks in it and piercing some body part—her nose ring was missing, too, come to think of it. She looked more like the girl her parents always wanted her to be.

"I know, right? Perfectly boring. The office demands"— she gave a dramatic sigh and made air quotes—"'human-colored hair and no facial piercings.'"

Sadie bumped her shoulder into Quinn's. "You couldn't be boring if you tried. You look amazing as usual, and I'm so happy to see you."

"Right back at you. Except you seriously need some ice cream. You're crazy skinny, girl!"

"Now you sound like Royce."

Quinn's eyes went comically wide. "I still can't believe you're working for him!" She clamped onto Sadie's arm and dragged her to one of the small round tables. "Tell me everything."

Sadie propped an elbow on the table and rested her chin in her hand. "I don't even know where to begin."

"How about how the hell you ended up working at Second Chance Ranch with your ex?" Quinn said it loud enough the employees and the few other people in the place glanced over at them.

"Is 'It's complicated' a good enough answer?" Sadie asked with a laugh. When Quinn folded her arms over the table, all business, she knew she'd end up spilling it all. So she filled her in, going into great detail so Quinn could help her analyze everything and figure out what to do.

"I bet he totally wants you again," Quinn said.

"Uh, no. Did you not hear the we-can-only-ever-be-friends part?"

Quinn waved off the comment, and that was when Sadie noticed the iceberg-sized diamond hanging on her necklace. The sun hit it and shined right in Sadie's eye. "Dang, Quinn, talk about bling." She leaned over the table and lifted it to inspect it. "Present to yourself, or is there a guy involved?"

"Well, you know how my sister's engaged? It's why I'm in town right now, actually—the wedding planning is about to commence, and trust me, the Sakatas know how to take all fun out of planning things. I give it five minutes until Maya's in tears and looking at me to fix it. Anyway, her fiancé's brother and I have been dating."

When Sadie let the necklace drop, Quinn tucked it into her shirt so that only the silver chain showed. "I think it's way too extravagant a present for where we're at, so I almost refused it, but then he looked so damn hopeful and it was big and shiny, so…" Her lips pursed and her eyebrows scrunched together. "I do like him. He's just already so serious about me, and serious in general—needless to say, my parents *love* him. I figure our siblings' wedding will either push us closer or screw it up. If it doesn't work, then Mr. Sparkles is definitely going back."

"You always did mesmerize the guys."

"Yeah, all the wrong ones. But I've changed my ways since high school. Now I go for the opposite of hot, tattooed, and totally unavailable. That's why Grayson might be good for me. I was going to tell you about him, but you'd just sent me that sad email with the news about your contract falling through, so…" She shrugged.

"You never have to hold back, you know that."

"I know. But, seriously, how are you holding up? The whole Royce thing aside?"

Over the past few weeks Sadie hadn't felt like lying in bed and never getting up again—well, she did some because working on the ranch was exhausting, but not in that sad, my-life-is-hopeless way. "The worst part was having my dream so close, only to get it yanked away. Just like when the girl group dissolved, only worse, because I thought I was finally going to sing the songs I wanted, my way. To have it fall through again made me question if I was any good. And when I couldn't even pull off a set I'd done a hundred times the very same day…well, then I was sure I wasn't."

"You are," Quinn said, covering Sadie's hand with hers. "You know you have a kick-ass voice."

"Thanks. And I do know. But I was never skinny enough or pretty enough, or big-boobed enough."

"Also bullshit. You've got perfect boobs that are never going to sag."

Sadie cracked a smile—she also noticed they were getting a few concerned looks now. Quinn had that effect on people sometimes, which was one reason why she loved her so much. "Man, I could've used you in Nashville with me. Don't worry, I'll stop wallowing soon, and once I get some money saved, I'll hit it hard again. Being here this past month has actually been a good distraction from it all, though. And now that you'll be in town more for wedding prep…?" She raised her eyebrows and Quinn nodded. "Good. Then I'm even better. Now, let's get some ice cream, already."

After they got their ice cream—and said hi to Mr. Hamilton, who'd asked a ton of questions—they sat to eat and finish catching up.

Quinn's phone rang, and she glanced at the display. "It's work. Sorry, I'll be just a minute." Whatever the person on the other end said set Quinn off. She shot out of her chair and headed to the corner, telling whoever it was that they better fix it and now, no excuses. She'd kill Sadie if she told her she sounded just like her father, even if it were true.

"Sadie, dear?"

Sadie glanced at Patsy Higgins. The woman was on every town committee ever, and somehow knew everything that happened within the town limits mere minutes after it happened. "Yes?"

"I ran into your mother and grandmother earlier, and they informed me you were in town for a while, and I got so excited because we've been missing our town singer ever since you left. We'd just be so honored to have you back."

Apprehension crept across Sadie's skin. Singing around the campfire was one thing, but she wasn't sure she was ready for a larger crowd. Of course, saying no wasn't really an option. Patsy Higgins didn't accept no for an answer—Sadie and Quinn used to joke that her grandmotherly exterior was a front to hide the fact that she was a former CIA spy who'd take you out if you didn't participate in town functions. Besides, a few low-key performances might be exactly what she needed to get her confidence back to where it needed to be. Then she'd be ready when she made her return to Nashville.

"Well, I'm honored to be back."

"Great! We've had to use a recording for the ball games and rodeos the past few years, and it always sounds all garbled and scratchy over the speakers. I'm so glad we'll have a stronger, more patriotic performance this Fourth of July."

"Wait? Fourth of July? As in—"

"The rodeo, silly! Good thing you don't need much prep time."

Patsy walked up to the counter and started rattling off her order. Sadie really should've seen that coming. So, on top of Royce roping and riding, she'd get to start the night with nothing but a microphone, her voice, and years of memories rushing her at once.

All the prep time in the world might not be enough.

• • •

Royce couldn't believe how bored he was. This far into the program, they let the kids have free time on Saturdays, and between them becoming pretty good workers and Sadie's help, he'd actually managed to catch up with things on the ranch. He could always find more to do, but that wasn't why he was bored. He didn't want to face the truth, but there it was, whispering in his mind.

He missed Sadie.

Missed watching her walk back and forth between working the horses and helping out with the teens. She was gaining weight—something he'd never tell her because he liked his balls where they were—and she was looking healthier, laughing more.

Royce pushed up the brim of his hat, pulled out his phone, and scrolled through his contacts, stopping on Sadie's name.

Don't do it. If he called her, what would he even say?

"Hey."

Royce almost dropped his phone. He quickly shoved it in his pocket and turned to Cory. "Yeah?"

"You and I are going out tonight."

"That sounds nice and all, but I—"

"Don't say you can't, man. You're starting to live like a monk. A cowboy monk, sure, but come on, it's getting pathetic. And I'm a young, good-looking guy. I shouldn't be wasting all this charm on horses and cows." Cory waggled his eyebrows.

Royce laughed and shook his head. "Dude, that doesn't

sound right."

"That just proves we need to get away from the ranch for a while. I already talked to your mom. Her friend Sheila's coming over to keep her company as soon as she gets off work at the diner, and Frank from down the road is on call if anything major happens."

Royce ran a finger across his bottom lip, tempted, but not sure if a night out was what he needed right now.

Hell, I need something to take the edge off wanting someone I shouldn't.

It was time to remind himself there were other girls besides Sadie.

Chapter Eight

There were two bars in town. One on the east end, closer to the fancy, bigger homes built or bought by people who'd come to Hope Springs to live off whatever fortune they'd acquired somewhere else. Quinn's parents fit that profile, and the Lounge definitely catered to them—it specialized in wines and colorful cocktails.

Bar number two was Seth's Steak and Saloon—generally referred to as the Triple S by locals—and it was the one you went to if you wanted the best steak in town, cheap but cold beer, and the chance to do some country dancing. People from other nearby small towns also frequented it, so it was also the best place to find a possible hookup. If Sadie knew Quinn—and she did—she'd be throwing cowboys at her all night.

There are worst things to have thrown at you, I suppose.

The front of the place stayed true to the look of old western saloons, although there were neon beer signs hanging in the windows. They sent flashes of colored light across Sadie's bare arms and legs. She'd put on her red smocked summer dress and paired it with her brown boots with the bright embroidered flowers. This afternoon, she and Quinn had ended up at the Curl Up and Dye Salon. Quinn had gotten a trim and a streak of red in the back that could be easily hidden—though she'd done her hair up in a high ponytail so it was showing now—and Sadie had the hairdresser take out her hair extensions. She'd also had her trim it so that it brushed her shoulders, and put strawberry lowlights into the hard-to-keep-up platinum blond. Thanks to the combination of her makeunder and having Quinn by her side all day, making her laugh so hard she'd had to retouch her mascara from crying, she felt more like herself than she had in a long time.

Quinn hooked her arm through Sadie's. "Okay, I'll save you if you give me the signal, but you should at least *attempt* to flirt with a couple guys. It's the only way you're going to move past Royce."

She almost said that she'd moved past Royce already. At one point, she had. Mostly. After being around him, though, she needed to re–get over him. If that were even possible. She took a deep breath. "I'll try. But you remember how many weirdos live around here. Not to mention I know too much dirt on most of them to ever consider them viable dating options."

"You haven't even talked to them, and you're already rejecting them."

"I'm sure your diamond-gifting boyfriend would be happy to know you're spending your evening scoping out dudes."

Quinn tugged her toward the entrance. "If he saw how much help you needed, he'd give me props for helping the helpless."

Sadie laughed and gave in, pulling open the door. The music was loud, honky-tonk vibrating through every inch of the place. They headed toward the bar to get drinks. The bartender's familiar face lit up with a smile.

"Sadie and Quinn, how the hell are ya?"

They leaned over the bar to hug Seth, one of their former classmates. "Your dad has you working for him, too?" Quinn asked.

"Nah, I just bought the place from him last year—so it's now technically Seth Junior's Steak and Saloon." He readjusted the faded green cap covering his red hair and jerked his chin at the jukebox. "Threatened to get rid of that and put tables on the dance floor, but there was an uproar. The town committee even wrote me a letter. Apparently the shit-kicking music and dancing must go on." He shrugged and then folded his arms on the bar. "So, what can I get you ladies to drink?"

They ordered two beers, and when they turned to find a table, Sadie nearly ran smack into Royce and Cory. She stopped so abruptly her drink sloshed over the glass and onto her fingers. She looked her ex-boyfriend–slash–boss up and down, taking in the Wranglers, black shirt with pearl buttons, and black felt cowboy hat. His eyes met hers and she forgot how to breathe.

"Now this looks like trouble if I've ever seen it," Cory said. Sadie could hear the smile in his voice, but she couldn't take her eyes off Royce. She was vaguely aware of Cory hugging Quinn. Then Quinn moved to hug Royce, and a pinch of jealousy went through Sadie's gut. Not because she thought anything would happen between Quinn and Royce, but because she'd never gotten a nice-to-see-you-again hug. They'd hardly touched since he'd run his fingers down her arm and squeezed her hand, and she'd relived it so much it was pathetic.

When Quinn stepped back, though, Royce's attention returned to Sadie. "You cut your hair." He stepped forward and picked up the ends. "You look like you again."

The strands slowly fell from his grasp, tickling her bare shoulder. His callused fingers brushed across her collarbone before he dropped his hand. Her skin was on fire. Probably as red as her dress. And she wanted more. Let it all burn.

Royce cleared his throat. "We should get that drink." He walked past her without another glance. Cory gave her and Quinn a quick smile and then headed after him.

Sadie followed Quinn to the closest table and dropped into a chair.

"Hol-ee hell!" Quinn slammed her glass down with a *clink*. "How can you say that boy doesn't want you anymore? I could *feel* the heat coming off you two."

Sadie glanced at Royce's back as he and Cory talked to Seth, and then she slumped down in her chair, tightly gripping her glass. "Well, apparently I'm not so scrawny that he won't check me out, but that's it. There's a difference between liking the way someone looks and wanting them."

"Oh, he wants you."

"You're talking sex, which is different from actually liking a person or getting involved in a relationship. Not that I'm looking for that right now."

I don't think I am, anyway. Not that it matters, since Royce made it clear he's not interested.

Sadie leaned forward and lowered her voice. "I know this sounds desperate, but I swear I'd just take the sex if I thought I could even get that." She took a generous swig of her beer. "Maybe we should leave. Watching him all night, seeing all the girls who'll inevitably hit on him, and the ones he'll hit on…that's not going to make me feel better."

"I think we just need to speed up the drinking." Quinn flagged the waitress who was walking by and asked for a couple shots of their best tequila.

• • •

Royce was doing his damnedest to not look at Sadie, but how was he supposed to do that when she was wearing that bright red dress? He'd nearly tripped over his own feet when he'd first seen those little strings that basically pointed to her cleavage. Then there was the way her hair skimmed her bare shoulders—strawberry-blond hair, the way she used to be. Not to mention the legs and the boots and the eyes and the lips. Even when he wasn't looking at her, he saw her.

He signaled Seth to ask for another drink.

"Obviously this plan didn't involve…" Cory gestured with his beer toward Sadie and Quinn. The other guys in the place were noticing the girls, too, which made it impossible to relax and enjoy this night away from the ranch. Every muscle in his body was tensed and the beer wasn't working near quick enough. When Seth placed a Coors in front of him, he asked for a shot of Jim Beam as well.

He caught a flash of red and gritted his teeth as Sadie hit the dance floor with one of the boys from the town over.

He couldn't remember the guy's name, but he was one of the Kendrick brothers. They were the pretty type who wore the cowboy uniform to go out but wouldn't know what to do with a horse if you handed them the reins.

Royce drank the whiskey as soon as Seth set it in front of him, letting it burn through him. "So this is getting out. It's not as fun as I remembered." He was pretty sure half the town thought he and Cory had some *Brokeback Mountain* thing going on. But if he needed to come out to the Triple S every weekend and pick up women to prove he preferred females, he'd rather just stay at the ranch and let them talk. What did he care?

"Dude, you can sulk, you can go find another girl to dance with, or you can grab Sadie for the next song," Cory said. "As for me, I've got a blonde with a low-cut top and, from the looks of it, even lower inhibitions staring at me, and I'm sick of living the monk life." He clapped Royce on the back and then headed over to the blonde. In no time, they were plastered together on the dance floor.

Sulk. He didn't sulk. He scanned the rest of the women in the place, determined to get Sadie out of his mind. But then he noticed her sit back down with Quinn. She leaned in and the two of them laughed. Warmth flooded his chest and he could feel himself smiling. It was nice to see her so happy. Hundreds of good memories pushed in on the corners of his mind. Since he'd dated Sadie, that meant he'd spent lots of time with Quinn, too. She was always fun, loud, and infinitely grounded, although that never stopped her from sneaking out of her house.

Sadie glanced his way, and he realized he was staring. He turned in his seat, focusing on the lights behind the bar and thinking he was completely failing at reminding himself other women besides Sadie existed. Obviously he was pretty rusty at this whole getting-out thing. There'd been a couple girls here and there, but it'd always ended with them complaining about how busy he was or how hard it was to get through to him.

Who has the time to deal with that? Ever since Dad died, he'd just worked, worked, and worked some more, so he could only imagine how much worse women would complain about his busy schedule now.

Maybe he should just go home. He was buzzing enough that he couldn't drive—Cory had driven anyway. But all of this wasn't worth the hassle, and if one more guy asked Sadie to dance…well, he was starting to feel like doing something stupid. Like going to ask her to dance himself.

And that would just make it too damn impossible to get the girl out of his head for good.

• • •

"Could you stop eye humping him and just go ask him to dance already?" Quinn tried to take a drink but was laughing too hard and ended up spilling it on her lap.

"You're still such a lightweight," Sadie said.

"I always hated I couldn't put it away like you. Guys are impressed with that."

"I'm not sure 'impressed' is the right word." Sadie took another sip, enjoying the buzz starting to form. "I can't drink like I used to, though. I spent too much time working, rehearsing, and filling every spare second with any performance I could get. Now I'm totally out of practice."

"I'll bet you the bill. If you go ask him to dance, I'll pay."

Sadie tilted her head. "There are some things money can't buy. Humiliating myself is one of them."

"Fifty bucks."

"That's just cruel. You know how broke I am."

Quinn tapped her purple nails on the top of the table. "That's why I'm offering. And adding in a double-dog dare you."

"You think elementary tricks are going to work on me?" Sadie looked from Quinn to Royce and back to Quinn. The current song ended, and another one started—quick, the kind that required someone who really knew how to country dance. And Royce did. "You're on." She pushed out her chair, tossing Quinn a smile. "You spoiled rich girls think you can throw money at anything."

Quinn laughed, then leaned forward and smacked her on the butt. "Go get 'em, tiger."

Desire was pressing her forward more than the bet— and okay, the liquid courage was helping quite a bit. It didn't keep her heart from pounding faster and harder with each step. Royce straightened, looking like he was getting ready to go.

All her words fell out of her head and all that came out was, "Uh…" She licked her lips and tried again. "Quinn says I don't know how to country dance anymore. Care to help me prove her wrong?"

As Royce pushed in the stool he'd been sitting on, his muscles and height hit her again. "I don't know that that's a good idea, Sadie."

A sharp pain shot through her chest. She'd told Quinn he'd say no, but she'd thought the bet would at least soften him, and the rejection firsthand—well, it sucked. "Oh. Right."

"I'll dance with you, sweetheart," the guy sitting a few spots down said. She wasn't really interested, but she supposed taking him up on the offer would help ease the sting. Anyway, put on a front that she wasn't so crushed by it, at least.

"On second thought," Royce said, wrapping his hand around hers, "I guess I can spare one dance." He tugged her toward the floor, slid his arm around her waist, and then gripped her hand tighter, holding it up in dancing position. One eyebrow quirked a little higher than the other, and there was a challenging glint in his eyes that reminded her of all the times they used to egg each other on. "Try to keep up."

Then they were off, feet shuffling, bodies spinning, trying to keep time with the music. She was rusty, and being drunk didn't help. But whenever she started to go the wrong way, Royce would nudge her in the right direction. Her desire for him flared hotter as he led, always in control, his strong hands on her. Sometimes it drove her crazy when he was bossy or argumentative, but she loved when he took charge of certain things. Dancing. Kissing.

Other things.

She gulped and her breaths were coming faster and faster, and not just from the dancing.

He spun her out, then twisted her tight to his side, both of them facing forward for a couple of steps. Another spin and she was in his arms, her chest pressed against his.

The song ended, the silence suddenly so obvious after the loud, and then Royce was pulling away. "Guess you remember enough," he said, and it took her a second to remember her excuse about how she needed to prove she could still country dance.

"Well, when you've got a partner who knows what he's doing, it helps."

A slow song started, and the couples on the dance floor reshuffled, some coming, some going. Royce took a step away, and she caught his arm. "One more."

"I—"

"Just one more dance." She gave his arm a gentle squeeze. "Please."

The tense line of his jaw softened and his fingers slowly curled around her hip. She kept the torturous space between them for a couple of eight counts, then moved in closer, until every inch possible was touching, and her hand was on his chest. With their bodies pressed together, the scent of his cologne filling her senses, and his intense gaze on her, she was back at prom all those years ago, the night he'd first told her he loved her. After the dance, they'd driven to the river, and one thing led to another. It'd been her first time, and she'd been surprised when he'd admitted it was his, too.

"Remember prom? Junior year?"

He didn't say he did, but his eyes finally met hers, telling her that he did and giving her enough courage to go further down memory lane with him. "We fell asleep under the stars, and then we got to wake up to your dad standing over us with a shovel," she said.

He smiled—a full, show-some-teeth smile. "I thought he was going to use that shovel to dig a hole so he could hide my body after he killed me."

Sadie laughed. "It was a close one—I don't think I've ever seen him so ominous-looking, not even with the kids from the camp. Good thing I was able to talk him down."

"Then you somehow convinced him to not call your mom and give you a chance to sneak home." Royce's smile widened, bringing out that sexy groove in his cheek. "What was your line? Something about how it was Second Chance Ranch, after all, and you'd be *so grateful* if he gave you a chance to not be grounded for life."

"I was surprised it actually worked," she said.

"That's because my dad always liked you—probably didn't hurt that you came and helped out with the animals all the time."

"Yeah, I was pretty proud of myself for being so convincing. Only then it ended up being all in vain, since my mom had already seen I wasn't in my bed, called the Sakatas and found out I wasn't staying the night with Quinn, and was about to call your parents when I showed up. Despite all the yelling, I remember thinking it was still one of the best nights of my life."

"It was a good night," Royce agreed, so quietly she barely heard it over the music.

She sank into his embrace a little more, feeling like there was too much space between them, even though they were connected as much as possible with clothes on. Royce swallowed hard, his eyes on hers. He leaned closer, his cowboy hat dipping down. Then, like her body was acting purely on instinct, she tipped onto her toes and kissed him.

She slid the hand she had on his chest up, behind his neck, and parted her lips. His hands pressed into her back, his tongue slipped in to meet hers, so familiar, yet new. He tasted like alcohol and mint and nights under the stars. Tingly heat traveled through her core. She could feel his body respond, knew they were making a spectacle on the dance floor, and she couldn't bring herself to care. Happiness bubbled up, making the heat spread faster, driving her to up the intensity of the kissing.

Then suddenly he pulled away, so fast she almost fell forward. Her arms were suddenly empty. Cold.

"Damn it, Sadie. You can't just come back and pretend everything's the same."

"I'm not. I get that things are different."

"You're right. This time, I'm not falling for it." He spun around and walked away, leaving her standing on the dance floor alone. He pushed out the door, and she forced her feet to move toward the bar area so she could find Quinn. Her lungs felt like they'd collapsed in on themselves, and every step was a challenge now that her limbs were dragging behind her instead of working the way they should.

Quinn and Cory were standing together, watching her as she approached. Quinn stepped forward and hugged her. "I'm sorry," she whispered.

Sadie looked to Cory, her view partially obscured by Quinn's hair. "He'll never forgive me, will he?"

Quinn dropped her arms and turned, looking at him like she wanted the answer, too.

Cory exhaled. "I don't know. He still cares about you. I think he's mad at himself for not being strong enough to stop caring. Just give it some time, and you two will figure something out."

Quinn wrapped an arm around Sadie's waist. "Come on. We're going to crash at my place tonight, and there's gonna be chocolate and more alcohol."

"I'll drop you guys off," Cory said. "That should give

Royce plenty of time to cool off before I go pick him up."

Sadie let her friends lead her outside. Numb, she climbed into Cory's truck. A hint of Royce's cologne hung in the air, and she was torn between inhaling and getting lost in the scent and covering her nose so she could try to forget it, along with this entire night.

As hard as she tried to stop them, the tears were forming, beginning to spill over. She thought about Cory saying she and Royce would figure something out.

She didn't want to wait for "something," though. Because she wasn't strong enough to stop caring, either.

Chapter Nine

Grandma was seated at the table making rolls when Sadie walked into the kitchen. The shower hadn't really helped her pounding headache, and the light streaming from the windows was far too bright. She and Quinn had stayed up until three a.m., but her stupid internal alarm clock was so used to getting up early for work now that she hadn't been able to sleep past seven, so she'd driven home and decided to get started on the day.

"Need some help?" Sadie asked, pulling out a chair.

Grandma pinched off a rounded piece of dough and set it next to the others. "Sure." She pushed the bowl of dough toward Sadie. For the most part, Grandma seemed to be doing well, but she tended to overdo it and then have a hard time moving the next day. Still, no one could convince her to stop cooking, and everything she made had to be done from scratch. Food was always the way to take care of people, and taking care of people was the way she showed her love.

"You'll never guess who was a hot topic at quilting this morning," Grandma said.

Sadie froze, a ball of dough in her palm. Several ladies got together Sunday mornings to quilt and basically discuss everything going on in everyone else's lives—big surprise, Patsy Higgins headed it up. "Please say it's because I'm singing at the rodeo."

"Oh, that was mentioned, but there was much more interest over you and Royce kissing at the Steak and Saloon."

Next to Grandma's perfectly shaped rolls, Sadie's looked lumpy, but she took her time putting it just so as she tried to figure out what to say. The reminder of the kiss sent an odd mix of hot and cold through her. It'd been such a great kiss—until he'd pulled away.

"Once you started working with him, I figured it wouldn't be long till you two were together again," Grandma said.

I'm gonna have to quit my job. I can't go to work and face him after that. "It was a mistake—one I wish the entire town didn't know about. We're not together. He'll never forgive me for leaving, and it's not like I can promise I'm going to stick around, even if he did."

"Oh, honey. I know you felt like you had to go to Nashville and try to become a famous singer, and I understand. There were times I used to wonder about what I missed out on. Especially when I was younger and people liked to tell me I hadn't really lived. I'd sometimes go to the city and be spellbound by all the stores and restaurants and flashing lights. But then I'd start to feel annoyed by how crowded and noisy it gets, and I don't have any need for flashing lights. After a couple-day visit, all I wanted was my little house with my bed and my kitchen arranged exactly how I like it. This simple life was a good fit for me."

"Simple? Grandma, you've worked harder in your life than most anyone I know. I remember how you used to get up at the crack of dawn to fix Grandpa and Mom and me huge breakfasts. Then you were always baking and helping out the neighbors and keeping this place clean. Not to mention how much you worked with the horses, too. You're kind of amazing, you know."

Grandma reached over and patted Sadie's hand. "Thank you, dear. Now I'm old and can hardly get out of my chair most days. I hate it."

"Give it some time. And if you need help, I'm here now."

"I'm so glad to have you home, but you were always such a star with that voice like an angel. I hate to see you give up—I know your mama sometimes wonders what would've happened if she would've pursued her opportunities, and sometimes I feel like I made a mistake not encouraging her more. Just know that you can be anything you set your mind to. Just decide what you want most, and I have no doubt you'll find a way to get it."

Being back in Hope Springs was proof that it wasn't exactly true, but she wasn't about to tell her grandma that she was wrong—that some things were practically unattainable, to the point she wasn't sure they were even possible. Royce was one of those things, and only time would tell if music was, too. Grandma's pep talk got her thinking once again about what Mom had given up, and even though she knew her mom was happy, she didn't want to live with regrets like that. The only way to ensure she never had a career in music was to quit, and she just couldn't let go of all the hard work she'd put in to get to where she was. She had to believe that after some time to recover, she could push herself to the next level if she gave it one more shot.

The back door swung open and Grandpa poked his head into the kitchen. "Sadie. Good, you're here. I could use a little help if you've got a minute."

Grandma nodded. "Go on. I got this."

Sadie headed outside to help Grandpa.

Grandpa handed her one end of the wire. "Guess who I picked up last night, apparently planning on walking all the way to Dixon Ranch?"

Sadie doubted he really wanted her to guess. She wanted to say it was Royce's own damn fault for being so stubborn, but she didn't have the energy. "You gave him a ride home, then?"

"Yep. Guess Cory was heading that way eventually, but I told Royce that I could use a drive, so he hopped on in. He was pretty quiet, though. Not that it's any of my business, but I heard you guys had been at the Triple S, so I thought you might wanna know he got home safe and sound."

After the falling-out, she'd worked to erase last night from her mind, so she hadn't really thought about it, but it was good to hear all the same.

Grandpa turned his attention back to the fence, asking her to pull the wire tighter as he secured it on the other post. She marveled at how he could still jump up on fences and the strength he possessed. She wondered if cowboys ever really retired. From what she'd seen, they didn't. They became part of their land and animals until there was no separating them.

Royce was a cowboy through and through. He'd told her having her at the ranch helped, and he looked less tired and stressed than he had when she'd first started working there. So maybe it'd be hard, and maybe there'd be no more kissing, but she couldn't quit on him.

Even if working at the ranch constantly reminded her of everything she'd sacrificed for her music.

. . .

Sadie walked out of the stalls and over to where most of the teens were gathered around watching something. As she neared the fence, she realized that Royce and Eli were on horses, practicing roping.

Funny how the kid claimed it was lame, and now he was racing across the land on a horse, lasso swinging over his head. He snagged the calf's head, and a few seconds later, Royce got the back hooves. They both glanced up at Cory perched up on the fence, who yelled out their time.

Royce and Eli jumped off the horses and went to work undoing the ropes.

Addison glanced at Sadie. "Royce told us we get to go to the rodeo if we're good these last few weeks, and I can't believe how excited I am for a *rodeo*. Also…" Her eyes moved to Eli as he draped the rope over his shoulder. "I never thought I'd say it, but cowboys are kinda hot."

Sadie crossed her forearms on the middle rung of the fence and watched Royce herd the calf toward the gate. His jeans were caked in dirt, and his hat was slightly crooked. "Amen, sister."

Addison looked at her, and she seemed to realize they'd actually agreed on something. Sadie wasn't sure who was more shocked. Come to think of it, they hadn't clashed as much lately. The chip on Addison's shoulder had lessened, along with her attitude, and the last time they'd brushed down horses, Sadie noticed Addison took great care to make sure the horse she usually rode got properly taken care of. She'd noticed Addison and Eli were pairing off now and then, too—never going far, since that wasn't allowed, but putting enough space between them and the rest of the group so they could chat without being overheard.

As opposed to Sadie and Royce. Their casual conversations were gone, although he was always polite. Distantly polite.

She'd been tempted to start a fight with him just so he'd show a little emotion around her. But they'd all been busy, and she supposed it was unfair for her to tell him not to be an ass to her only to pick at him until he broke. This past week had definitely been a lot longer than most, especially with Quinn back in Cheyenne, not due to visit again until the rodeo.

The buzz of a motorcycle broke through the sound of the horses and the conversations going on around her. The black bike pulled up in front of Royce's cabin, and Royce ducked between the gaps in the fence and headed over to talk to the guy. Caroline called the kids for lunch, but Sadie hung back, wondering if she should saddle up one of the horses and ride to the river. Maybe that'd help clear her head.

Only then her stomach growled, reminding her how long ago breakfast was. She'd have to take her ride later this afternoon, after her work was done—Royce didn't seem to mind her taking the horses out whenever. Not like he'd actually talk to her if he did. But they needed exercise, anyway, and it got her away from him, so she figured he counted that as a bonus.

Whoever was on the motorcycle buzzed back down the driveway, and Royce headed toward the cabins, which meant they were going to have to be near each other without a bunch of people between them.

Not talking seemed weird, and honestly, keeping her mouth closed just wasn't in her skill set, so she asked, "Who was that?"

"You remember Heath Brantley?"

The guy had been in the class two years ahead of theirs and had a motorcycle, tattoos, and piercings—basically he was the town bad boy. She was pretty sure he played guitar for some band, too, so add that to the irresistible-to-women category. "He's still around here?" She looked in the direction he'd gone, even though he was too far away now to make out any details. "Pretty sure every woman with eyes remembers him."

Royce gave her a sidelong look, a hint of annoyance in his features.

"Quinn was the one with the mad crush on him. I had you, so…" He tensed, and, as she had many times before, she wished for the ability to stuff words back in her mouth. Instead, she blurted out more to try to keep the conversation going. "What was he doing here? Motivational speaker for the kids?" she joked.

"He's moving back to town, apparently. You remember Mountain Ridge Bed and Breakfast just down the road?"

She nodded. "Yeah. Quinn always talked about how sad it was that it was just sitting there getting more and more run-down. She even said that someday she was going to restore it—we actually broke in one night to check it out."

Royce ran his fingers across the stubble on his jaw, and

Sadie got a little lost in the motion. "Well, rumor is the family's finally going to put the land up for sale. Heath wants to buy it, and since it borders the ranch, he wanted to discuss plans and make sure it works for what we've got going here. We set up a meeting for later in the week."

"That was nice of him to check with you."

"Apparently the town committee gets to vote on what happens to it, since it's been declared a historical site. A lot of the older ladies were sure he belonged here at the alternative camp—or in jail—so I think he wants me to help convince them to let him buy it. Apparently I'm upstanding enough to be a good personal reference."

Right before they reached the cabins, Royce gripped her elbow, pulling her to a stop. Between the tense eyebrows and the way his mouth tightened, she knew it was going to be bad.

"Don't say it. I can't hear it again. I know I screwed up, and I'm trying to give you your space, but I hate that I've pushed you to the point that you completely ignore me, and—"

"Like ignoring you is even a possibility." A hint of a smile ghosted across his lips. "I was actually going to ask if you wanted to ride up with me and Cory to a horse sale in Rawlins this afternoon."

It took her brain several seconds to process the words. An hour and a half each way with her seated between Royce and Cory in a truck? Or maybe they'd take the extended cab and she'd sit in the back alone. Yeah, that was probably more the way he'd go.

"If you've got other plans, no worries," he said. "We won't get back till late, but you've got a good eye for horses and their dispositions, so I could use your opinion."

His hand was still on her elbow, warming the skin there, and he was so deliciously dirty from roping. "I'd love to go."

"All right, then." He gave one sharp nod and dropped his hand. "Let's get some food and then we'll take off."

. . .

Royce figured having Cory with them would act as a safe barrier between him and Sadie—a barrier that he was coming dangerously close to breaking every time he looked at her. The truth was, he couldn't stop thinking about that kiss on the dance floor.

He'd meant what he said about her having a good eye for horses, but he'd also decided he was distracted enough wondering about her, he might as well have her with him. And this way, he'd be in control of the situation. Only the horse trailer had already been attached to the single-cab truck, and there was no way Cory was going to straddle the gearshift, which meant Sadie ended up right next to him, her thigh against his and her light floral perfume impossible to escape.

"That's enough classic rock for one day," Sadie said, switching the radio to a country station as if she owned it, just like in high school.

"Hey, I like classic rock." Royce reached for the buttons.

"How many times have I told you? That's just cowboy blasphemy!" Sadie shoved his hand away. "It's a good thing I'm here to help you see the light."

He lifted his hand toward the radio again, and she grabbed onto his wrist and yanked his arm down. She raised an eyebrow at him, and he was tempted to show her how easily he could overpower her. That'd mean not having her hand on his arm, though, and he was enjoying the way she'd grip it tighter every time he made the smallest movement.

"Ooh, I love this one!" she yelled as a new song started, and, holding his arm tightly with one hand, she cranked up the music even louder with the other.

Since it meant her smiling, bopping in her seat, and singing, he'd always let her control over the radio slide. He supposed the bopping around was still cute enough—and heaven help him, her voice never failed to unravel him. As she was singing "She Ain't Right," he thought it was the perfect song for her. Except that'd be him admitting that she was just right for him.

She nudged him. "Cory's singing, and I'm singing. Stop being a fuddy-duddy and sing with us."

He rested his wrist on the steering wheel and glanced at her. "Fuddy-duddy?"

She leaned in and sang, her face so close to his that he almost forgot to pay attention to the road. He shook his head. She poked a finger at his cheek. "I'm gonna do this the entire way unless you sing. Come on. Sing. I know you've got a perfectly good voice."

"The voice is okay, it's being on key that I've always had trouble with."

"Whatever." She poked his cheek again, so he sighed and then went ahead and sang a few lines. She looked so proud of herself that he couldn't help returning her smile. Although he'd never admit it out loud—because he'd never hear the end of it if he did—he liked that she pushed him to remember how much fun the little things could be. For so long all he'd been focused on was work and fixing problems, and it was nice to relax a bit. Now that he thought about it, it was probably the other reason he'd asked her to come today.

After the song ended, Sadie turned to Cory. "So, let's talk ladies, Cory. Where you at with them these days?"

"I'm a fan."

She giggled. "But is there a special girl? You know, I could try to set you up." Her eyebrows drew together. "If I knew any girls who lived here."

"And therein lies the problem," Cory said. "There aren't a whole lot to choose from. Besides, the bachelor life suits me just fine. I'm looking for fun more than serious."

"Lame!" Sadie crossed her arms. "I'm not setting you up with any of my nonexistent friends now."

"Damn," Cory said, snapping his fingers, and she laughed again, the sound echoing through Royce's chest.

Then she turned to him, opening her mouth like she was going to ask him something—possibly the same thing—then thought better of it. Which was good. No way he was talking women or dating with her.

Especially not with that one line from the song repeating in his head over and over. *She's just right for me.*

He pulled up to the grounds where the horse sell was going on and got out of the truck. They got a pamphlet with all of the horses listed and walked through, checking them out in person as they read off their stats.

Cory split off to look at a dun mare, and Royce headed over to the stallions. When they got to a tall buckskin, he glanced at Sadie. "This was the one that caught my eye when I was scanning through the list."

The horse ambled over and stuck his head over the gate,

sniffing at Sadie. She patted his head. "Well, he's definitely not shy."

Royce knew there were people who were good with animals, but he couldn't believe the way all of them seemed to automatically trust Sadie. She was already talking to the horse, her voice calm as she told him how pretty he was and that he was "Such a good horsey."

She put her hands on either side of his face and peered into his big eyes. "I think I love him."

"What about his build? He's got good strong muscles in his legs, but sixteen hands? He's a little on the tall side for roping. I also gotta think about the birthrates and if the height will cause a problem for my mares."

Sadie jumped up on the gate and ran her hands down the horse's neck as she studied him, her lips twitching one way and then the other. The horse kept bumping his nose into her, wanting more attention. Royce wasn't sure he needed a horse that followed her around like a puppy, but it was pretty damn endearing.

"Tall and lean, but he's still got the muscles for the quick start roping requires, so I think you'd be good. Just a sec." She pulled out her phone and took a picture and then sent a text. "Now we'll see if my lessons to my grandpa on how to text paid off."

They were still standing in front of the pen when her phone rang.

"That's him. Maybe I failed at the texting lesson." She answered, and her face lit up as she talked to him. Her grandpa was one of the best guys Royce knew, not to mention he also had a sixth sense when it came to horses. Royce knew that in a lot of ways, Gene Manning was more

Sadie's dad than her actual dad. All in all, she and her father had a good relationship, but Gene was the man who'd really raised her.

She hung up and spun around. "He said he approves. You know I'm attached now, right? Me and"—she took the pamphlet out of Royce's hand and read off the name—"Duke are destined to hang out more."

"Destined, huh?"

A grin curved her lips, and she nodded enthusiastically. "Written in the stars and shit."

Royce laughed and then held out a hand to her. "Looks like we gotta go see a man about a horse, then."

She gave an adorable little squeal, slapped her hand in his, and jumped down. Her body bumped his, and for a moment they froze like that, the same way they'd done on the dance floor, and he was thinking about that kiss again.

Pushing her away the other night had taken all his strength, and right now he wasn't sure why he was bothering to hold back, or if he even wanted to. This time around, there were no illusions of rodeo wins with Sadie by his side and a family in the future. He knew they had different goals that'd eventually take them down different paths.

Actually, he was sure that what he wanted to do was take her to bed and work out the tension between them. He'd sworn he'd never let his life get so wrapped up in another person again, and he was planning on sticking to that. But he could keep his feelings in check, just like he'd done for years.

"Did you de— Never mind." Cory turned to go in the other direction, and Royce let go of Sadie.

"We're gonna go make an offer, actually," Royce said. "Sadie claims she and Duke are destined to be friends, and I don't know how to argue with that kind of logic."

"The answer is simple. You can't." Sadie gripped his hand and headed toward the entrance. He pulled against her a little—just so she didn't go thinking she was in charge. Plus, there was the added benefit of the view of her butt in the tight jeans she had on.

Cory raised his eyebrows in a silent question as they passed him. Royce shrugged, and then he went to buy a horse for a girl who might not even stick around long enough to help take care of it.

Chapter Ten

When Royce got done loading Duke into the trailer, he went to find Sadie. He found her tossing horseshoes with a boy who couldn't be more than five or six. She was also laughing, that loud, infectious, head-turning laugh that drew people to her wherever she went.

She glanced up as he approached. "This kid's a horseshoe hustler! I just lost five bucks!"

The kid grinned up at her. His white hat was big enough it wobbled on his head. He gathered up the horseshoes and looked at Royce. "Would you like to play, sir?"

He was going to say that was okay, but Sadie grabbed his arm and yanked him closer. "You've got to see this. It's like that trick-shot kid who beats all the celebrities at making baskets. Deacon makes amazing tosses instead. He's like a machine. A pint-sized, accurate machine."

Royce took the horseshoes from the kid—Deacon, apparently.

"One point for close, two for a leaner, three for a ringer."
Deacon gestured for Royce to go first.

His toss was a little too far.

Deacon grinned and threw. The horseshoe clanged
against the spike—a ringer. His grin widened.

Sadie placed her hand on Royce's shoulder and leaned
in so her body was against his back, and tucked her chin on
her hand. "Isn't he the cutest?"

Royce glanced over his shoulder at her. "He's pretty
damn cute."

She shoved him forward. "Okay, go again."

He got one leaner, one point for coming close, and—
finally—a ringer. But the kid had thrown all ringers, and
as the last one fell over Royce's, he glanced up and said,
"Mister, that means my ringer cancels yers. But good try."

Patronized by a grade-school cowboy. Royce laughed and
handed over five dollars. Deacon shoved it into his pocket.
"Why don't you two play? You could use the practice."

"No, I—"

"Good idea," Sadie said over the top of him, gathering
up the horseshoes. "Royce is much closer to my level, and
I could use a win after you wiped the floor with me." Her
eyebrows scrunched up, her tongue came out, and she kept
swinging her arm backward and forward over and over,
before finally letting the first one loose.

Her tosses were all over the place. Close and then way
over. Short and long. As usual, though, she just grinned or
laughed her way through each success and failure, bouncing
on the balls of her feet, energy radiating off her. Her last toss
hit and leaned against the spike. She pumped her fist and
then turned and high-fived the kid.

Royce didn't bother pointing out that he was already so far ahead that it didn't matter. He swung back to throw, and as his arm came forward, Sadie pinched his butt. The throw went wild, not even in the pit, and her laughter bordered on maniacal.

"You cheater!"

Instead of responding to the accusation, she said, "I'm starving, and there are hamburgers over there. And since my ethics were a little blurry there at the end, I'll buy."

"Pretty sure food is provided."

She innocently batted her eyes at him, told Deacon that he was awesome, and then walked over to the table with the food. Royce headed to the truck to see if Cory was back — he'd texted a bit ago to say he was gonna check out a few more horses.

While Royce was next to the trailer, he peeked in on Duke. *He does look like a good roping horse, and with his long legs, he can eat up that space fast.* Chevy was always his go-to, but she was getting older, and he might want to get another colt out of her in a few years.

Balancing a stack of hamburgers in one hand, Sadie lowered the three pops she had under her other arm into the back of the truck. She set one off to the side — for Cory, he assumed — and then extended a hamburger to Royce as he neared. "Mustard only, though I still think it's suspect to not like ketchup."

She sat on the open tailgate, her legs swinging through the air within seconds — she never could sit still.

Royce bumped her over with his hip and settled next to her. "Tomatoes are disgusting, no matter what else you add to them."

"They're good for the prostate—people are always talking about it on the news."

"My prostate's just fine, thanks."

Her gaze dipped down, focused right on the zipper to his pants. Her legs stopped swinging and she sank her teeth into her bottom lip.

Liquid hot lust swirled through him, and he gripped the edge of the tailgate with his free hand, working to calm it down—they were in public, after all. "Eyes are up here, darlin'."

Pink spread across her cheeks, but she shrugged and laughed it off. Too bad he couldn't do the same thing, especially when she leaned her head on his shoulder— the girl had serious boundary issues. Not that he bothered putting more space between them.

They finished their food and cracked open the cold Cokes to wash it down.

"This makes me think of all the rodeos we went to," Sadie said. "Chevy in the trailer, picking up food whenever we could." She turned her face up, and the sun highlighted the freckles on the bridge of her nose—he was glad she'd stopped covering them with so much makeup. "Whenever I used to get to missing home real bad, I'd go to YouTube and watch rodeo clips. It was like comfort and torture, all at the same time."

Her voice caught, and he reached over and threaded his fingers through hers. She squeezed his hand as if she were afraid it'd float away—or maybe that she would—if she didn't hang onto it. "I don't want to ruin this…awesomeness we've got going on today, but I don't want to repeat past mistakes, either." She let out a long exhale. "The truth is, I have no idea how long I'll be in Hope Springs."

"I figured as much. It's not really like you to give up on somethin' you've set your mind to." Knowing it and having her tell him were two different things, but it was a good reminder that this was all temporary. Now he was the one squeezing her hand like it'd disappear any moment.

"My manager told me he'd call if he got any interest, and in theory he's still looking for opportunities for me to perform, but I'm not holding my breath. That's why I'll need to head back eventually—my odds go way up when I'm constantly performing where the right person might hear me. I just needed some time off, and I'm not sure how long it'll take until I feel ready and have enough money saved to return to Nashville."

Tucking a leg under her, she turned to face him. "I'll admit I took the job on the ranch because I was desperate, but like I told you before, I love it there, and I'll try to give you as much notice as I can."

"I understand."

She nodded, dropping her chin for a moment before slowly looking back up at him. "You know, now that I've seen what you've done with the ranch and the camp...well, it was already hard enough not to compare every other guy to you. I always did, and they always came up short." She ran her hand down the side of his face. "You're one of a kind, Royce Dixon."

He nearly groaned at the brush of her fingertips across his lips. "There's no one quite like you, either."

She tilted her head, one corner of her mouth turning up. "That explains why we were so awesome together." She brushed her fingers across his bottom lip again, grinning when he gently nipped at them. "I might not be staying in Hope Springs forever, but I think it's a damn shame to not have some fun while we can."

"Is that right?" He'd been thinking the same thing, but if she was going to keep trying to convince him, he wasn't going to stop her.

She leaned closer, her breasts pushing against his arm, her warm breath on his neck. "We could go out under the stars, just like old times…"

He tried to swallow.

Her hand moved over his heart, which was now steadily picking up speed, and then she curled his shirt into her fist and gave a light tug. "Come on, cowboy, don't say it hasn't crossed your mind."

He kept trying to come up with words to say, but his brain and mouth were having a disconnect. So he crashed his mouth down over hers. She made a little gasp noise, and he took advantage, deepening the kiss, taking her stolen breath in and letting himself get lost in the feel of her soft lips, the familiar taste of her tongue.

He was half tempted to take her right here in the back of the truck, despite all the people nearby—the horse trailer mostly hid them, after all.

There was a small whispering in the back of his mind that they were gonna make a mess of things, but with her draping her legs across his lap and her nails running over his back, he couldn't help thinking that— Well, actually it was more like he couldn't actually think at all.

• • •

As they headed back to Hope Springs, Duke and a sorrel quarter horse named Flint that Cory had bought in the trailer behind them, the radio played in the background, and Royce's hand remained firmly wrapped around Sadie's thigh. She leaned her head on his shoulder, soaking in how amazing it felt for him to not fight her anymore.

Grandma did say I could get anything I set my mind on. She probably hadn't meant seducing her ex, but the entire afternoon, all Sadie could think about was how much she wanted him, and she'd be lying if she said it wasn't empowering.

They hadn't made a big announcement to Cory or anything, but the second he'd seen them sitting in the back of the truck, talking with their faces close together, he'd raised an eyebrow that said he knew.

The nearer they got to the ranch, the hotter the desire pumping through her body became. After weeks of longing, her anticipation was a living, breathing thing, taking over every inch of her body.

They'd sneaked off together countless times in high school, but it'd been so long, and she was definitely out of practice. *Crap, does my underwear even match?*

Royce tapped his fingers to the beat, each hit causing her pulse to scatter in a dozen different directions. As he turned in to the ranch, though, his fingers stilled and he swore under his breath.

Sadie straightened and peered out the windshield. "What's wrong?"

Royce pointed his chin toward the girls' cabin. The porch light was weak, but now she could make out Caroline standing with her hands on her hips. Eli and Addison stood across from her. "That doesn't look good."

The truck lurched to a stop, and Royce was out the door in seconds, long strides eating up the space between the truck and the kids.

"I'm gonna get the horses situated," Cory said.

Sadie climbed down from the truck, the pins-and-needles sensation in her butt and thighs slowing her steps. By the time she got close enough to hear, Royce's voice was raised—firm yet deadly calm—kind of like a great white shark swimming by. No need to attack when all those teeth were on display.

"...know the rules! You'll both be missing the rodeo."

"What? No!" The words were out of her mouth, so loud in the air, and the opposite of calm, before she could stop them.

Royce whipped his head toward her, jaw clenched, and she froze. Now he was a shark sensing blood in the water. "Sadie, go help Cory with the horses while I take care of this."

She stepped forward, placing her hand on his arm. "But—"

"Now."

Normally she'd scowl and tell him not to boss her around, but she could tell she'd crossed a line, and honestly, she was terrified he'd go back to pushing her away if she fought him on this. So she cast Addison and Eli a last look—her heart ached when she saw the sorrow on their faces. Even Addison, whom she'd never thought she'd be defending. Then she turned and headed toward the stalls.

As she was walking away, she heard Eli saying it was his idea, so to just punish him. Her feet revolted at taking her farther, but she forced them to go anyway.

She and Cory were just finished getting the new horses hay when Royce came in. His super-serious and super-grouchy expression was still in place.

"Need me to stay in the cabin?" Cory asked.

Royce took off his hat, stuck it on a post, and sighed. The band had left a slight indentation, and his hair was adorably crumpled, though she knew better than to say so. "No, I'll do it—you go on home and rest up so one of us can be awake tomorrow. My mom's watching both doors right now so that I can shower and grab some bedding, and then she'll stay with the girls tonight."

"I'll see you tomorrow bright and early, then." Cory clapped Royce on the back. "Best of luck."

As soon as Cory was gone, Royce turned to Sadie. She flinched, already knowing she was about to get into trouble. "You can't undermine me like that in front of them."

"I'm sorry," Sadie said. "But they're just a couple of kids with crushes on each other, and they were both so excited about the rodeo." Eli had even sketched pictures with a rodeo theme, asking her if he'd gotten them right. "Seems too harsh to take that away from them."

Royce took a step toward her, and she crossed her arms in front of herself as she brought up her shoulders.

"Jeez, you think I'm gonna attack you or something?"

"I've never seen you look so scary before."

He put his hands on her hips, and her muscles slowly relaxed. "When it comes to the rules, I have to be harsh. Do you know how hard it'd be to get credibility back if those kids got their hands on drugs or had sex? Or even tripped and hurt themselves this late at night while they were unsupervised? Mom and I have to *constantly* do paperwork and reports and fight to keep all the checks and balances taken care of."

"I get it, I do, but…think of us back in high school. We were always sneaking out late, going for walks, looking at the stars…"

"Getting naked in the back of my truck." He ran his gaze down her and heat pooled low in her stomach. "I *am* thinking about that. And that's the problem. I know all too well what happens when two teens wander off alone."

"What *can* happen. We dated for a long time before we had sex. And I know not everyone waits, but — "

Royce kissed her softly, a gentle, way-too-short press of his lips, gone before she could fully catch hold. "You're clearly too soft for this side of things. I love that you care so much, but I'm doing it because I care, too, and it means I'm spending at least tonight in the cabin with the guys to make sure no one sneaks out again. In other words, it's gonna be a long night, and I'm already exhausted."

Sadie stuck out her lips in a pout as all her plans for tonight flew out the window.

Royce ran a knuckle down her cheek. "I'll see you tomorrow morning, and then we'll figure out when you and I can sneak away."

Gripping a handful of his shirt, she yanked him to her. She kissed him with all the built-up frustration inside her and drew it out, gently biting his lower lip. He groaned, and she moved her lips to his ear. "The longer you make me wait, the harder I'm gonna make you work for it."

Chapter Eleven

Sadie's shoulder was starting to burn from throwing the lasso over and over again. She was bad enough at roping when the object didn't move. Royce was going to use Thor for the Fourth of July rodeo but said the horse needed more practice and he was too busy to do it. He claimed it was more about the horse getting used to charging after the calf—without breaking the barrier, of course, or a ten-second penalty would be added—and knowing when to pull back, not so much her throws landing true.

Which was good, because she was zero for ten. A few of the teens had lined up, which only amplified her frustration every time she failed to catch anything but dirt. Addison and Eli were missing—apparently they'd had to wake up at six a.m. to start mucking stalls.

Taking in a deep breath, Sadie gripped her rope and nodded at Mark. He pulled the lever to let the calf out of the chute. As soon as it reached the end of the tether, Sadie kicked her heels into Thor's side, swinging the rope through the air. She leaned forward, aimed for the head, and released.

The lasso hit the hindquarters of the calf before falling to the ground. Sadie dismounted, anyway, to at least go through the motions of tying up the imaginary cow.

"Your timing's way off."

She turned to see Royce coming over the fence.

"Thank you, Captain Obvious. Now let me be Queen I Told You So and remind you that I clearly stated I was no good at this. *You're* the one who insisted it didn't matter if I missed."

"Well, I didn't think you'd miss every time. I don't want Thor thinking that's the goal." Royce flashed her a teasing smile, and she smacked his arm. "You're not pulling back right, either. If the calf's actually caught, Thor needs to keep the tension in the rope. He knows better, but you've got to yank back and remind him sometimes."

"Why don't you take over, then, and I'll do whatever you're doing?"

"I'm babysitting Addison and Eli and making sure they don't talk to each other. I think we've already established you're not built for that job."

"You've got them shoveling crap all day, and they can't even talk to each other? That's, like, *beyond* mean."

Royce pressed his mouth into a tight line, his expression saying, *This is exactly what I'm talking about.* He took the rope from her and put his hand on the small of her back, guiding her over to Thor. "Come on. I'll show you. We've got to get him out of the gate faster, too."

"Are you ever going to let them talk again?" she asked, glancing over her shoulder at him. "They only have a little more than two weeks left, and they like each other. They're good for each other."

"I know you have a soft spot for Eli, but—"

"You have one for Addison, too, so I don't understand why you won't at least consider the fact that this is a different-from-the-norm situation and give them a break."

Royce threw his head back and sighed. "I explained last night, Sadie. Soft spots don't change anything." He tugged Thor's reins. "Now, focus on the roping. No cowpoke of mine is going to get away with not knowing how to lasso a calf."

Sadie crossed her arms. "I'm just your cowpoke now? Am I not allowed to have an opinion?"

"Not at this moment, no." He pushed her toward Thor again, and even though she'd climbed on all by herself plenty of times before, Royce apparently thought she needed a boost, via a hand on her butt. Then he swung himself behind her, the leather of the saddle creaking under them, and it was hard to hold on to her irritation at him. Especially when his heat was seeping into her, his thighs against hers.

Royce handed her the rope, the loop already set. Instead of letting go, his fingers curled around hers. "Tell the truth. Are you missing on purpose since you're pro-calf?"

Sadie bit back a smile. "I wish I could use that excuse. It's starting to make me angry that I can't at least get one, actually. And I'm even more impressed that you make it look so easy."

He pressed a kiss to the spot just under her ear, the sensation of his lips so unexpected that goose bumps broke out over her entire body. "Thanks, darlin'." He wrapped an arm around her waist and covered her hand holding the rope with his. "Now, just feel it."

"I'm feeling things, all right."

Royce's fingers twitched, tightening their grip. He cleared his throat and then nudged the horse into place. When Mark tripped the lever to open the chute, a reddish-brown calf shot out, full speed.

The world sped up and slowed down, a blur of sensations going through her at once. She felt Royce's body, firm behind hers, his hand guiding the rotation of her wrist. Thor darted forward, the way he never had when only she was on, the rapid beat of his hooves drowning out all other sounds.

"Let," Royce whispered in her ear, "go."

The rope soared through the air, and for a moment, Sadie thought it was going to land in front of the calf, but it caught the head—a bit crookedly—then slid down. Thor automatically pulled back, yanking the rope tight, and Royce practically shoved her off the horse.

"Hurry!" he yelled, putting the other cord of rope in her hands.

She rushed over and tried to flip the cow to the ground. But it didn't want to flip and it was mooing like crazy, so she just looked to Royce as he came over.

"You gotta throw your body into it." He flipped the calf with ease, and she watched the muscles in his body work as he held it in place. "Now bind the feet."

Sadie glanced from the noisy cow to Royce's face.

"You're not going to do it, are you?"

She wrinkled her nose and shook her head.

"Be careful as you take the rope off, then. Don't get kicked. You know, the whole reason we do this for competition is because it keeps us sharp when we need to give the cows their shots or check their hooves. Or if we've got one that needs something, like—" He pointed to the ear tag.

"Earrings?" she said in her best ditzy voice, slipping the rope off the calf's head.

The corners of Royce's mouth twitched. "Yes, most cattlemen are concerned their cows aren't fashionable enough."

The calf mooed and took off running in the other direction. A whistle cut through, and the teens by the fence were cheering, so Sadie gave a dramatic curtsy. When she straightened, she expected Royce to sigh or shake his head at her.

Instead, he shot her a smile and ran his fingers down her arm until their hands were linked. "As far as rodeos are concerned, I think you'd better stick to singing and looking pretty."

She leaned in and whispered, "How about the part where I congratulate the rodeo winner in private?"

Royce's grip on her tightened. "Woman, I'm pretty sure you're going to be the death of me."

• • •

Royce had no doubt Sadie thought she was being covert, but he'd seen her eyeing the horse stalls since lunch, and he knew it was only a matter of time before she went to check on Eli and Addison. Which was fine if that was all she was going to do. He had a sneaking suspicion, though, that those extra cookies she'd taken during their snack break weren't for her.

Balance had always been a problem with him and Sadie,

and she'd always had too much power over him. He was never letting another woman do that to him, least of all the one who'd screwed him up in the first place.

When he opened the door to the barn, Sadie was next to Eli, and they were both smiling. Addison was eating a cookie, talking to the two of them with wide, animated eyes, and it looked like Sadie had just handed over an extra-large cookie to Eli. Royce looked at Cory, who shrugged. He'd taken over the afternoon babysitting shift. They'd made the kids start at opposite ends, and not only clean out the pens but do all fresh straw. It was a hard five-person job. As a two-person job, it was the kind of awful that made seconds stretch to hours. In fact, if you looked up "most horrible job" on the internet, mucking stalls was on top.

Both Eli and Addison were dirt covered, clearly exhausted. As they should be. Tonight they'd crash instead of sneaking out.

"Cory, take Eli and Addison to the cabins." He addressed the kids. "Ten minutes to shower and change, and then you need to report to Mrs. Dixon for kitchen duty." He eyed the woman who was currently driving him crazy. "Sadie and I need to have a chat."

They put away their tools and practically ran outside.

Once they were alone, Royce turned to Sadie.

She twisted a strand of hair around her finger. "It was just a cookie. I was careful not to say anything that'd undermine you."

"You coming to see them and smuggling them dessert does undermine me."

"I heard you earlier, okay?" She walked toward him and put her hand on his arm. "You have to be strict, and

I get that, I do. But it was their first offense, and I was just thinking that if they got a little cheering up, then—"

"This isn't like in high school, where you can just smile and bat your eyes and get your way."

"I didn't do that."

"All the time." He'd constantly caved because she was damn cute when she batted her eyes or pouted to get her way. But after they broke up, he'd realized she'd had all the control, all the time. "I was a pushover then, but I'm not anymore. And our…arrangement aside, I'm the boss, and I know what I'm doing."

Her jaw clenched. "Being the boss doesn't mean you ignore your employees' opinions."

"If you'd like an official meeting, we can set up a time to discuss it. You don't go behind my back, and you don't argue with me in front of everyone, the way you did earlier today. We can have fun, but we need to maintain a professional working relationship. I won't be pushed around or persuaded by your over-the-top flirting or even sex."

She dropped her hand from his arm. "Yeah, I don't think sex will be part of the equation."

"Well, you do what you've gotta do. But when it comes to giving in on this subject, it's not gonna be me."

Sadie made a *pffht* noise. "We'll see about that." The challenge in her voice made it clear she didn't think he could hold out.

He advanced on her until her back was against the wall. "Yes, we will." He ground his hips against hers and she bit her lip. Then he was thinking that he should be the one biting it.

Desire flooded his veins, but he took a deep breath and

tempted his resolve by leaning against her and gently biting the lobe of her ear. "Make sure to let me know when you've changed your mind."

Her sharp intake of breath sent satisfaction through him. He took a moment to soak in her half-closed lids, flushed cheeks, and how her body felt against his. Then, even though it meant his night would be going in the opposite direction he wanted it to, he spun around and left.

Chapter Twelve

Sadie crawled underneath the covers and tried to fall asleep. Only sleep wouldn't come, and she couldn't get comfortable, and just *ugh*!

This whole sex-off thing she and Royce were having was ridiculous. It'd been two days of him brushing his hand across her skin every time he passed. Of tipping his hat at her and winking. Today he'd even resorted to whispering dirty things in her ear.

How can he lecture me about maintaining a professional work environment when he's the one feeling me up every day?

She'd wanted to have an actual meeting to talk about Eli and Addison having at least the hope of going to the rodeo, but she wasn't sure she could be alone with Royce without throwing herself at him, and if he said no to her suggestion about the rodeo…

Well, she wanted to say she could hold out until he could be reasonable, but she was seconds from caving as it was.

Sadie had thought a lot about what he'd said, though, and although she hated to admit it, even to herself, there were times in high school when she'd used the way he felt about her to get her way. But it was always more of a constant push and pull between them, if you asked her. They'd still argued plenty, and the last thing she'd call him was a pushover.

Flipping onto her side, she fluffed her pillow and tried to shut off her brain so she could actually get some sleep. But then she was thinking about the time they'd broken up for a week when they were teenagers. One of their arguments had gotten out of control, they'd said things they didn't mean, and they were both too stubborn to admit it. He certainly hadn't let her bat her eyes to get out of that fight.

How did *we get over that one?*

After a moment, she recalled the night at the Dairy Freeze—where all the great high school drama went down. Quinn had convinced her to go to the ball game, and they were there, along with the team, celebrating their win. Quite a few guys from Green River's team were there, too, and Quinn was telling her that if she wasn't going to call Royce and make up with him, she should go find a rebound guy among the football players so she'd stop being "so sappy sad all the time."

Sadie had just started talking to one of the Green River boys when he'd yanked her to him, gripped her butt with both of his hands, and tried to kiss her. She'd shoved him hard in the chest and said, "Get off me."

He reached for her again, but then Royce was there between them. She wasn't sure when he'd walked in, but he was more pissed than she'd ever seen him. The muscles in his entire body were coiled as if he were ready to pounce, and an angry vein throbbed in his forehead. "Touch her one more time, and you'll never use that hand again."

She grabbed Royce's elbow. "I have it under control."

"That's not what it looked like to me."

Anger flared up in her, and she went from holding his elbow to smacking his biceps. "I'm fine. And you can't keep all guys from talking to me forever." Earlier at school she'd been laughing with a few of the football players, and at one look from Royce, they'd backed away.

Royce turned to face her. "Sure I can. I plan on it, too." He stepped closer and lowered his voice. "Come on, Sadie. Stop being so damn stubborn already."

"Your apologies need serious work, Royce Dixon." She turned to storm away, planning on telling Quinn she wanted to go. Now.

Royce's arms came around her waist. She knew it was him instantly, the way her body reacted to him, his woodsy cologne mixed with the sweet smell of hay.

"Everyone's staring," she said, hating that her shaky voice gave away her crumbling resolve so easily.

Royce's breath hit her ear, and a shiver ran down her spine. "I'm sure they are. I'm also sure I don't care." Her pulse quickened, and she was having trouble remembering why they'd broken up. Some fight over…something stupid. She let herself lean back, into his warmth.

That was all it took for him to haul her out of the shop. He deposited her inside his truck, climbed in after her, and cupped her cheek. "I love you, Sadie. I'm sorry that I implied you're not as physically strong as me, okay? This week has been awful, and I miss you like crazy, and I just want us to be good again." His eyes locked onto hers, and the passion in them sent fire through her entire body. "Is that a good enough apology?"

She licked her dry lips. "I miss you, too. And you know I love you. It's always gonna be you."

Relief flooded his features, then he was pulling her onto his lap, wrapping his arms around her, kissing her like he intended to make up for all the kisses they'd missed that week.

See, she thought as her body sank deeper into her mattress. *I didn't always get my way. And pushover guys don't go around carrying girls out of ice-cream shops.*

Tomorrow, she was going to make sure to bring that up to get her way.

• • •

When Sadie awoke, she struggled to get a grasp of the time and place. Everything seemed off, and it took her a moment to realize her cell was buzzing on the side table and must be what woke her up, considering it was still pitch-black outside her crooked red curtains.

She picked up her phone and smiled when she saw Royce's name on the display, along with the fact that it was nearly one thirty in the morning. She connected the call and said, "Booty calls at this time are *definitely* admitting defeat."

"It's Chevy. She's having her foal, but something's wrong, and I can't get ahold of the vet."

Sadie flung off her covers and grabbed a pair of jeans.

"I don't know what to do," Royce said, and she could hear the worry in his voice. "She won't stand still, and she's obviously struggling, and—"

"Hang tight. I'll be there as soon as I can."

• • •

Royce heard the door of the barn open, then Sadie was rushing over, and the tight knot in his chest loosened a little.

"Sorry to call so late," he said as she slipped into the stall where Chevy was alternating rolling on her side and stomach, her breath coming out in heavy bursts. "I've seen dozens of foals be born, and even helped, but…"

Sadie put her hand on his arm. "But this is Chevy. I get it." She gave his arm a quick squeeze and carefully approached the horse. "Hey, baby. How you doing?"

Chevy rolled onto her side again and grunted. Sadie dropped down in the straw and ran her hand over the horse's neck and side.

For the first time since Royce had found Chevy dancing around—before she'd been getting up and down and rolling around—she calmed a bit, her legs no longer kicking out. Getting Sadie over here had definitely been the right call. He knew her presence would help settle the horse down and that she'd know what to do, just like he was sure having her by his side would keep him from panicking.

He'd repeatedly told himself to remain calm, that horses gave birth all the time, but this was *his* horse. The first horse he and Dad had trained from birth. He'd ridden her for years, and they'd done countless rodeos together. They were a team, and he needed her to be okay.

His throat tightened as he watched the translucent white sac appear and disappear. The horse was pushing, but there wasn't any progress. Chevy trembled, her heaving breaths and grunts loud in the quiet night. His gut told him it'd been too long. Something was wrong.

"I think its feet are hung up," Royce said. "I might have to pull it."

Sadie glanced over the horse's body at him. "I'll try to keep her calm." She ran her hand over Chevy, telling her she was a good girl and praising her efforts.

With the horse's next push, Royce caught the feet. Nope, not feet. Just one foot. The other must be stuck. Keeping hold of the one, he searched for the other. Everything was slippery, and it was dark, and then the one hoof he'd had hold of was sucked back in again.

"Can you come grab the flashlight?" he asked. "I can't see a damn thing."

Sadie slowly made her way over, running her hand across Chevy the entire way as she continued to coo at her. She squatted next to Royce and shined the flashlight on the tail. The next time the hoof broke free, he reached in again. This time, he found the other one and guided them out.

He gave Chevy a few minutes to rest, and when she pushed again, he pulled. The foal's nose appeared, and he tugged again, using every ounce of strength he had to get the front half of the horse out.

Just as he was about to tell Sadie to get the sac off the baby's face, she reached forward and tore it, peeling it from the horse's nose. The little thing clambered into her before settling onto the straw, ribs rising and falling with its breaths, its back half not quite free.

Royce released a long exhale, his tension leaking out with it. "I think they're out of trouble now." He scooted back to the corner to give Chevy space, and Sadie came and sat beside him.

Over the next few minutes, they watched as Chevy finished pushing. The baby horse stuck out its front legs, tried to stand, and wobbled back down. Sadie made a little *aww* noise and he smiled at her.

Her gaze met his, and he wrapped an arm around her shoulders and curled her to him. He hugged her tightly, and she kissed his cheek. "Pretty impressive, cowboy," she whispered, and happiness and affection warmed him from the inside out.

They stayed until Chevy stood and broke the umbilical cord, and the baby—a good-sized filly that looked just like her dad—took a few wobbly steps.

Sadie yawned and shook her head as though she was trying to keep herself awake.

Royce ran his hand down her back. "It's too late for you to drive home, especially as tired as you are. Why don't you stay at my place tonight?"

She sleepily bobbed her head as another yawn took over. "Okay." She glanced down at her clothes. "I could use a shower, too."

"I've got one of those," he said with a smile. Then he stood and held out his hand, a lightness filling him when she took it.

• • •

The shower had taken the edge off her sleepiness, and Sadie suddenly found herself in severe need of a glass of chocolate milk. She rolled up the sleeves of the flannel shirt Royce had given her and padded to the kitchen.

"If I were a can of Nesquik, where would I be?" She opened cupboards and found plates and cups. The next one revealed soup and canned fruit and vegetables, but no chocolate powder.

He might not have any.

She decided to try one more cupboard, but it was the high one, and she had to stretch onto her toes. *Yes!* she thought when she spied the yellow container with the bunny on the front. She stretched farther, trying to get purchase on it. *Almost...*

"Need help?"

The canister tipped and she ducked her head as it fell. It crashed against the counter and chocolate powder exploded everywhere. She coughed, waving away the brown cloud in the air. "Sorry," she said, glancing over her shoulder at Royce. "I didn't know you were there."

Her heart stuttered when she took in his damp hair and the sheen of water on his bare skin. He had on low-slung drawstring pants and nothing else. The temperature steadily rose and she had to force her attention back to the task at hand. Using the side of her palm, she swept the spilled powder into a pile.

"It's okay. Just leave it." Royce's hand came down on her shoulder. "I see you still have a chocolate milk habit."

Her tongue suddenly felt too big for her mouth. "Yeah, when I was on stupid diets all the time, it was the one thing I could never cut, no matter how hard I tried."

"It's stupid you were ever even on a diet. You were perfect the way you were." He spun her around, and then his gaze dipped down to his too-big shirt on her. "The way you are now." He reached up and slowly undid the top button, and then the next one. Her heart beat wildly in her chest, and her skin tingled every time his fingers brushed it.

Light-headedness was taking over, and addictive shivers of energy were traveling down her core. "Is this where you demand I admit defeat?"

His eyebrows drew together, then understanding dawned on his features and his forehead smoothed. "No. This is where I thank you for helping me tonight." Everything inside her unraveled as he undid the button at her navel.

"Besides saying it with your mouth?" Her voice came out as shaky as she felt.

"My mouth will definitely be involved." He dipped his head and licked at the chocolate powder dusting her collarbone. Then his tongue dipped lower, and a moan escaped her lips. She grabbed his hips and pulled him closer. His mouth captured hers, and he boosted her onto the counter, sending the open container of Nesquik to the floor.

She wrapped her legs around his waist until he was firmly against her, and then deepened the kiss, tangling her tongue with his. Heat built between them as she ran her hands over the muscles in his arms, across his shoulders, down his back.

He slid her shirt the rest of the way off, leaning back for a moment to study her. "Definitely perfect," he said, then he was lifting her into his arms and walking through the house. He kicked the door of his bedroom closed behind them and gently lowered her to the bed.

She tugged him to her, kissing her way across his chest, and then moving to his firm abs. He moaned, and she smiled against his skin before gripping the waistband of his pants and sliding them down. Everything was familiar but new, and so many years had lapsed since their last time, it felt like it was their first all over again.

And she planned on taking her time rediscovering every. Single. Inch.

Chapter Thirteen

Royce's heart expanded as he took in Sadie's sleeping form, so still in sleep. He traced the line of her back with his fingers, marveling at how soft her skin was.

His eyes burned from being open for so long, and the red numbers of his bedside clock blurred together as he tried to make out the time.

I really should get up and check on Chevy and her foal. Leaving the comfort of the bed was the last thing he wanted to do, though, especially with the girl he was falling for all over again sleeping next to him.

He'd tried to stop himself from getting attached, but how could he, when everything felt right when he was with her? He kissed her bare shoulder, inhaling the soapy and chocolate scents on her skin. When he'd walked in on her getting the Nesquik, stretching far enough to make it clear she wasn't wearing any underwear, he knew he was a goner. And now here he was watching her sleep.

This entire situation had a good chance of ending badly. She'd made it clear that all she could offer was fun—and while she'd certainly delivered on that, he found himself wishing for more. For years he'd told himself he was stupid to ever want to settle down at the age of nineteen. That he was glad it hadn't happened and probably never would. But something about being with Sadie made him think about how he still wanted that.

With a girl who didn't.

Shit. He rolled onto his back and looked through the skylight at the stars dotting the dark sky. He had to figure out a way to keep this situation from getting out of control. Careful to not wake Sadie, he dragged himself out of bed and immediately missed her skin against his. He covered her with the blanket, despite his desire to stare at her naked body for a few more hours, then pulled on clothes and headed out to the barn.

The filly was up and sucking, and Chevy looked back to herself. "You did good, girl." He got her some grain and then headed to the boys' cabin to do a check on them—Mom was sleeping in the girls' cabin again tonight, just to make sure there was no more sneaking out for at least one set of kids. Sadie would probably accuse him of being sexist, but the girls were the ones who could get pregnant, so that was both his and Mom's reasoning. He could only be in so many places at once.

When Sadie leaves, we'll be shorthanded again, and I'll be back in the at-risk situation I was in before she stormed back into my life. Not to mention I'll be bored out of my mind.

Unless she decides to stay…

He clenched his jaw and shook his head. He knew better

than to waste time wishing for things he couldn't have.

The guys were accounted for, so he went back inside and slid into bed next to Sadie, telling himself to just enjoy it while she was here, and, even if it went against every instinct he had, to not think about the future.

• • •

When Sadie rolled over, the bed was empty where Royce had been, and bright morning light poured in from the skylight. She loved that his bedroom was set up to lie back and look at the stars at night. Despite how tired Sadie was, the sunny blue sky was a nice sight, too.

Everything was more wonderful than it'd ever been, actually. She could feel the smile stretching her lips, and the memory of last night made her body tingle from head to toe. She and Royce were as good together as she remembered and then some.

Clutching the sheet to her chest, she swung her feet to the floor, searching for her clothes—or more accurately, Royce's shirt. Except then she remembered she'd lost that in the kitchen. The rest of her clothes were probably still on the bathroom floor.

"Mornin'," Royce said, stepping into the doorway of his room wearing only his jeans.

Sadie's skin hummed as she stared at him. "Morning."

He reached up and gripped the top of the door frame. "If you need to take today off, or if you wanna go home and come back later…or if you just want to stay here and rest, you can do that, too."

The words seemed far away. She was too focused on the

way the muscles in his arms and chest were standing out with him gripping the doorway like that to pay attention to what he was saying. Sunlight streamed through the room, clinging to him like it wanted him as much as she did. She'd never understood girls calling a guy beautiful before, but as rugged as Royce was, she couldn't help thinking that right now, *beautiful* described him perfectly.

He raised an eyebrow. "Sadie?"

"Huh?"

A slow smile spread across his face. He closed the distance between them and leaned down to kiss her.

She dropped the sheet and pulled him closer.

He made a low noise in the back of his throat. "I can't. Cory and my mom already covered for me this morning, and I've got a ton to do today."

"Starting with me?" she asked in her most innocent voice, batting her eyes.

He wound his fingers through her hair, tilted her head back, and brushed his lips against hers. "Ending with you, if you're good."

Reluctantly, she let go of him, and he moved to his dresser, put on a shirt—which was just a shame—and then tossed her one.

She stood and stuck her arms through the sleeves. "How're Chevy and the baby?"

"They both look great. Been trying to think of what to call the foal, but I think I've named too many horses over the years. Nothing's coming." He finished buttoning his shirt and then his dark eyes met hers. "You should think of one."

"Are you serious?" Her voice came out several octaves higher than usual, excitement taking over. He wanted her to name a horse?

"If you want to, go for it. But nothing I'll be embarrassed to call her."

"Twinkle Toes it is."

He shook his head and grabbed his cowboy hat off the dresser. "You're going to make me regret this, aren't you?" He gave her another kiss as he brushed past her, stuck his hat on his head, and then walked down the hall, his boots echoing against the hardwood floor.

Sadie leaned against the door frame, basking in the euphoric haze winding its way through her body.

It was funny how the life she was sure she didn't want when she was a teenager was starting to look more and more like perfection.

• • •

Sadie found Grandpa in the kitchen, a jar of green olives in his hand. He extended them to her, and she grabbed a fork, dug a couple out, and popped them in her mouth.

"Chocolate milk?" he asked.

"Yes, please. But I can get it." Sadie busied herself with making it, humming as she did. She'd come home for a quick rest and a shower and was getting ready to head back to the ranch. Royce wouldn't tell her what he'd planned, only to dress warm.

"You seem happy," Grandpa said, and she smiled at him.

"I am. Last night I got to see a baby horse come into the world." It was one of the most incredible things she'd ever witnessed, giving her a rush similar to the one she got when she was onstage singing. She couldn't stop thinking about the way she and Royce had sat after he'd pulled the foal, his arms around her as they watched the miracle of life unfold right before their eyes. "Royce said I get to name it. It's black like Casanova, and I'm thinking Shadow. That's a good name for a black horse, right?"

"I like it." Grandpa dug into the jar for more olives. "So, if you're naming horses...sounds like you and Royce are getting pretty close again? Not that it's any of my business."

It cracked her up how Grandpa asked questions and then immediately followed them up by saying it wasn't his business, like he was curious but thought he shouldn't be.

"We are. I'm sure there's about to be a whole lot of gossip in town about us, and some of it might actually be true." She leaned against the counter next to Grandpa and knocked back her chocolate milk. All day she'd walked around with a big goofy grin on her face. "He's a good guy. I can't help but like him."

Admitting it out loud was nice. A little scary, too, because she worried she was getting in too deep. They'd agreed they'd just have fun, but it felt like it was morphing. Becoming more.

After everything they'd been through, she wondered if they truly had a chance at a real relationship.

Now I'm getting ahead of myself again. No reason to turn all serious when things are working the way they are. But suddenly she found herself thinking it wouldn't be so bad if it took her a while to figure out how to get back to Nashville. A longer reprieve might be better for her in the long run, especially if it meant more time with Royce.

"Well, he's a good kid. And I'm sure having you help out has been nice for him. I worried he was running himself ragged. Not that it's any of my business."

"Don't worry, I plan on making sure he doesn't run himself ragged." Sadie hugged Grandpa and kissed his cheek. "I'm off, and I might…" Even though she was an adult, admitting to a sleepover made her feel like a teenager all over again. "I might stay with Royce tonight."

"Drive careful."

Sadie set down her glass and was halfway through the living room when Grandpa called her name. He walked over and took her cell phone out of his pocket. "I nearly forgot. Your phone kept ringing over and over. I figured it must be an emergency, so I answered. Some guy named Nolan Martin wants you to call him."

"Nolan?" *Why is my agent calling?*

"Said you'd know who he was, and that he'd left a message already."

She took the phone from Grandpa and stared at the display. One message and three texts telling her to call him. For the past few years, she'd always rushed to answer, hoping for good news. Usually it was bad, with the occasional good mixed in. Now she just stared, not sure she could handle whatever it was he had to say. "Thanks," she choked out.

On the way to the truck, she checked the message. In true Nolan fashion, it was nice and vague: "Give me a call, Sadie. Got some exciting news."

When it came to her agent, that could be anything from a nonpaying gig at a bar to auditioning for a label to he'd found a doctor who'd give her a discount on the boob job he still thought she should have.

Curiosity ate at her the entire drive to the ranch, but every time she picked up her phone to call back, she ended up not going through with it. She told herself that it was because it was now late in Nashville, but Nolan would probably still be awake. Really, it was more about making sure she had a perfect night with Royce before she dealt with whatever her agent threw at her.

She told herself she was just being overly paranoid, but she suddenly felt like the clock was about to strike midnight, and once it did, everything in her life was going to change.

Chapter Fourteen

Royce had just finished saddling Duke when Sadie drove up and got out of the truck. She glanced over at him with the horses and then dove across the bench of the truck, giving him a nice view of the rhinestones on the back pockets of her jeans. When she came back out, she was holding a pale straw cowboy hat. She stuck it on as she approached, and it was the cutest damn thing he'd ever seen.

She wrapped her arms around his waist and tipped onto her toes to kiss him. He pulled her tight against him, sliding his hands into the pockets he'd been admiring. All day he'd had a hard time focusing on his work, counting down the minutes until he could kiss her the way he wanted to.

When they came up for air, he handed her Duke's reins. "Time to fulfill your destiny." He climbed onto Thor and glanced over at Sadie, now atop Duke.

"I thought of a name for Chevy's foal," Sadie said, and Royce automatically braced himself. She nudged his leg with the toe of her boot. "Hey, have a little faith."

"Seeing as how you did suggest Twinkle Toes earlier, you could understand why I'm a bit worried."

Her lips curved into a grin, and he thought it might be a mistake letting her name a horse that'd stick around longer than she would. "I was thinking Shadow. You haven't had one of those already, have you?"

"Nope, and I like it." He tightened his grip on the reins. "Ready?"

Sadie nodded.

"Same place as usual? Unless you think that horse you picked out can't keep up?"

"Oh, prepare to eat our dust, cowboy."

He opened his mouth to do a little more trash-talking, but Sadie kicked Duke into motion.

Cheating as usual, he thought, taking off at a gallop after her. It'd been a long time since he'd ridden with reckless abandon, all fun instead of rushing to fix something or being completely focused on training the horse on the quick start that roping required.

Sadie rode low to the horse, her excited yells trailing behind her—regardless of what she thought, she was a cowgirl at heart. There was no way she could ride like that otherwise. In a couple large strides, Thor caught up to Duke, and they raced across the land toward the setting sun that was turning the sky orange and pink, neck and neck the entire way.

Last minute, Sadie eased ahead, Duke's long legs giving her the edge, especially combined with the fact that Thor was trained for fast bursts instead of distance.

She jumped off and whooped and hollered, throwing

her hands in the air. Her cheeks were wind whipped and her hat had blown off, hanging on by the string around her neck. Her strawberry-blond hair swirled around her face in the light breeze, messy and sexy as hell.

Duke nudged her shoulder, and she turned around and ran her hand down his nose, praising him. "Don't you wanna congratulate me?" she asked Royce as he neared, a smug expression on her face.

"For cheating? Sure, congrats on winning by cheating," he teased.

Her mouth dropped open and then she smacked his arm. "Sore loser."

"Sexy siren."

She grinned at that and then blew him a kiss. They walked their horses into the heavily treed area they used to visit all the time in high school and secured them to lower branches so they could graze. They'd chosen this spot because it had perfect coverage from people if they happened by—which was rare, and so far, only during the day—with the leaves overhead still sparse enough to see the stars.

Royce got to work building a fire. Every time he glanced up, Sadie's hungry eyes were on him, and it was all he could do to not say, *Screw eating; let's skip to dessert.*

He laid out a blanket close enough to get the warmth of the fire, but not so close it'd get burned, and pulled the foil dinners out of his saddlebag. They chatted and relaxed while the food roasted. By the time they finished eating, the fire was dying, so he got up and added another couple of logs.

When he sat down again, Sadie settled between his thighs, her back against his chest. He ran his hands down her arms and then intertwined their fingers. "You good?"

She twisted her head and kissed his jaw. "Really good." She smiled, but then that faraway look she'd gotten off and on all night crossed her pretty features. It reminded him of the look she got whenever she talked about singing.

"Tell me about Nashville," he said. Part of him knew he didn't want to hear it, but he also needed to see how she talked about it, and he found himself wanting to know what she'd been through. Why things hadn't worked out yet.

"Where to even start...?" She dragged the heel of her boot back and forth in the dirt, creating a groove in the soft powder. "It was hard at first. I had no idea what I was doing, and I missed home. I missed you. Like, I'd-cut-off-an-appendage missed you."

He smiled at that, but his fingers also twitched around hers as that same feeling he'd gotten at the horse sale hit him—of needing to hold on before she floated away.

"But I was also fascinated with the city and the endless possibilities, and I made myself go all in, no looking back. No calling you like I wanted to." She glanced up at him with such tenderness that he felt the residual ache of wanting to talk to her and no longer being able to. "I knew the music business was competitive, but I had no idea just how competitive or how soul crushing it could be. I just wanted to sing, you know? Even though every rejection stung, I learned from them, and then I started making progress..."

She mentioned booking singing venues, landing an agent, the group she was briefly in, and how it'd ended because the other two girls couldn't get along. "It sucked, but I'd gotten to record in a studio, and it led to other opportunities. I opened for a few big-name artists, and when Tyler Blue was inducted into the Louisiana Music Hall of Fame, I got to fly to Louisiana and sing one of Blue's covers right before they took the stage—my agent's their agent, so it was something he set up, but still, the energy of the hometown venue, and all those people..."

Her eyes lit up, and he was suddenly jealous of everyone who'd heard her. "One of the best moments of my life, hands down," she said. "I told myself it wouldn't be long before a crowd like that would show up for me.

"Then I got the call that I'd always dreamed about. An exec at Downhome Records heard one of my demos and wanted to sign me. I quit my job, bought these boots"—she lifted her foot, the fancy pattern on her shoe now covered in dust—"and called Quinn and my family to tell them it'd finally happened. That I was going to sign a contract."

The firelight danced in her eyes as she stared into the flames. "My agent and I went to the Downhome offices, and I thought it was just to sign the contract, but then this guy in a suit comes in and says he's sorry to have wasted our time, but they'd signed a few other female singers over the past week, and when it came down to it, I just didn't have that unique spark that'd set me apart from the already crowded female market.

"My agent got all fired up, but my body went numb, my dream bubble popping as the words 'no unique spark' played over and over in my mind."

Royce's heart tugged, and he wrapped his arms around her. "That's total horseshit." He couldn't believe it. Did they even pay attention when she sang? He listened to the radio plenty, and to say Sadie wasn't unique—she was different and amazing, and all the record label people were idiots.

She blinked back tears and shook her head. "Whatever,

you know? It happens. Then, to make everything a hundred times worse, I had a breakdown during my next performance. Even though I'd sung at that club all the time, my confidence was shot. I screwed up right at the beginning, and then I kept thinking, *This is why the contract fell through.* So I started crying and"—she winced—"ran off the stage. After that, I pretty much hit rock bottom. And I just knew it was time for me to come home."

The way she called Hope Springs *home* gave Royce a glimmer of hope for her staying long-term. But then he registered the sorrow and regret in her voice. It dug at him, making him want things that were at complete odds with each other.

"I guess all of those ups and downs ended up making me who I am, right?" Sadie continued. "I experienced things people only ever dream of and realized I was stronger than I ever thought I could be. I tell myself that I got farther than most people do, so I shouldn't feel like a failure, but it kills me that it still wasn't enough."

He kissed her temple, leaving his lips on her soft skin as he spoke. "I'm sorry, babe. But I know how driven you are, and you've got the most amazing voice I've ever heard. You'll bounce back, stronger than ever."

She shrugged. "At first I thought having to move home was the end of the world, and all I could think about was how I was going to get back to Nashville as soon as possible. But it's nice to see my mom—even though she's busy as ever, something I swore I was going to help fix—and I can chat with my grandpa about anything, and he just gets me. Then I get to sit across from my grandma as she tries to teach me to cook, and I start thinking it's a good thing I came home for a while, and that maybe I shouldn't rush. I'd regret not spending more time with her if her health takes a turn for the worse instead of better. You just never know when it might be your last chance."

Sadie suddenly stiffened and twisted to face him. "Sorry. You lost your dad, and here I am talking about how great it is to have my family. I wasn't thinking."

"It's okay for you to talk about spending time with the people you love, Sadie."

She ran her hand down his chest, resting it over the hollow spot that opened up whenever he started missing Dad, as if she knew right where his soul needed soothing.

"I constantly think about how lucky I was to have spent so much time with my dad before he died," he said. "Giving up rodeos sucked at first, but I knew he needed the help, and with him, work didn't feel like work. If I'd been on the road all the time, I would've missed it."

"I should've been there for you—I knew how close you were to him, and he was…" Her voice came out rough and her bottom lip quivered. He could see her fighting her emotions, and it made it hard to hold back his. "He was always so good to me, like I was part of the family already." Unshed tears glistened in her eyes. "I wanted to come back when I heard, but I figured you wouldn't want to see me."

Just the fact that she cared that much about his dad and had even thought about it comforted him. Made him not feel so stupid for everything that'd happened in the past, or for thinking they had a shot at turning their current relationship into something more than just temporary fun.

"You shouldn't have gone through that alone," she whispered.

Royce swept her hair off her face. "I had my mom. It was a shock, and it was hard, but we got through it." There were days where it felt like they were still getting through it, and plenty where the grief would push its way up when he least expected it. But he knew he needed to be strong for Mom, and it helped that he could reflect on all the hours working with Dad, and how much he'd taught him over the years. That he could look out at the land Dad had loved and see hints of him everywhere.

Sadie sniffed. "Sorry, I didn't realize I'd get so emotional." She grabbed his hand and sandwiched it between hers. "Anyway, I honestly don't know how you manage to do it all, but he'd be proud of the way you've handled everything. You're kind of an amazing guy, Royce Dixon." She peered into his eyes, and her forehead wrinkled like she was trying to work out a math equation. "How did you manage to stay single?"

"It's not too hard. Just work all the time. A lot of women can't handle that. They want a show cowboy, not a real one."

"Not me."

"Oh, yeah?" He leaned closer until their breaths mingled.

"Yeah. I want a rodeo clown."

He shook his head and then captured her lips with his, cutting her laugh short as he pulled her onto his lap.

She brushed her lips across his and then placed a light kiss on them. "You know, it is okay to take a break once in a while. Maybe put an extra week between camps so you're not working yourself quite so hard?"

He shrugged. "Maybe."

"And speaking of Second Chance Ranch...I really don't

want to start a fight, but just hear me out, okay?"

He sighed, sure he wasn't going to like where this was going. "Okay."

"So I get that Addison and Eli broke the rules, but they've been working like crazy for the past few days, and they don't have very long left at the camp. I think what they need is a spark of hope. Like, say they had a..." She made a big of show of tapping her finger to her lip, acting like she was just now trying to come up with an idea, even though he knew where this was going. "I know! A rodeo! Something they've *never* been to before and thought was lame, but now they realize how cool it'd be, and if they had that goal to work toward, they'd still see that they made bad choices, but they'd keep making *good* ones so that they could go."

He stared at her raised eyebrows, the hope shining from those green eyes that she was definitely batting. He'd sworn he wouldn't be a pushover, but he supposed he had been a little harsh on two kids who were doing something he and Sadie had done several times when they were their age. Maybe he'd overcompensated by being harsh so he'd prove that she had no control over his decisions, which was laughable. Clearly she knew it, too. "I'll consider it."

She grinned and even clapped. Then she dove onto him and attack kissed him, starting with his lips, moving across his jaw and neck, and then back to his mouth. He lay back on the blanket, pulling her with him. Every few minutes, one of them would lose an article of clothing, until there was nothing and yet everything between them.

• • •

Sadie tried to hold back a shiver, but her body shuddered anyway. "It's colder than I remember."

Royce tugged the blanket up and held her closer. She rested her head on his chest and ran a hand down his stomach, trying to curl every inch of herself around him. Hopefully his warmth would soak into her, and soon. Apparently she'd gotten too used to Nashville temperatures.

He rubbed his hands over her arms, heating her skin with his deliciously callused palms. She grinned up at him and he smiled right back, like they were in on some secret that was all theirs. And they were. This was their special place with their very own starry sky overhead, and the only thing that mattered in the world was here and now. She wanted to capture the bliss wrapped around her like a second blanket and hold it next to her forever. It was all so perfect it almost seemed like a dream.

The ring of her cell phone broke through the sound of the nearby rushing river and popping fire. She bit her lip, wanting to ignore it, sure Nolan was calling again—she should've known he'd keep calling.

Maybe it's Mom or Grandpa or Grandma, though. She felt around for her phone and then looked at it. She was right the first time. She glanced at Royce and decided whatever it was, she could deal with it better with him next to her.

"Sorry. Just give me a minute." She pulled on her shirt so she wouldn't freeze and answered her phone, thinking she might be too late to catch it before it rolled over to voicemail.

"Sadie. Didn't you get my message?"

"Don't you ever sleep?"

"Not when I'm sitting on news like this. Remember the hall of fame ceremony when you did that cover of 'Next

Time' before Blue went onstage?"

Since it was pretty much the most awesome moment in her singing life, she thought it was a silly question. *Of course* she remembered. "Yeah."

"Well, one of the junior executives from Belle Meade Records heard you sing, and apparently you made a big impression. Now that she's been promoted, she wants to meet with you. They've already agreed to fly you out, but it needs to be this weekend. As in, you need to fly here tomorrow afternoon so we can meet with them first thing Saturday."

Excitement danced through her stomach. Belle Meade was *huge*!

But then she glanced at Royce, watching her with his steady gaze, and confusion crept in. A month ago, she wouldn't have thought twice about jumping all over an offer like this. It was everything she'd worked for for six years. All the tears, the heartbreak—it might actually pay off.

But what would she lose in return?

Everything's still so new between us, though. It's not like... She almost thought it wasn't like she loved Royce, but her heart filled up with all of their memories, old and new, and she knew that wasn't true. *I do love him. I'm not sure I ever fell out of love with him.*

Royce sat up, the blanket falling to his waist. He grabbed her hand, squeezed it, and mouthed, "Everything okay?"

"Sadie?" Nolan asked.

"Um, can I call you back? Like tomorrow morning?"

"We need to jump on this now, Sadie. Remember what happened last time? This is a fickle business, and if you don't grab onto an opportunity, you might lose it."

Cold spread through her gut. She clenched the phone tighter. Clenched Royce's hand tighter. Her dreams were within reach but in danger of slipping between her fingers, and she wasn't sure which dream to hold onto.

Country star?

Starting a life with an amazing horse rancher?

"I'll call you first thing tomorrow, I swear." Sadie hung up and twisted to Royce. She could see all the questions in his eyes. If only she knew how to answer them.

"It was my agent. A record exec from Belle Meade wants me to go sing for her this weekend." She swallowed. "It's…well, it's unbelievable, really. But I'm not sure what to do. I don't want to leave you in the lurch with the ranch."

The ranch? Why'd she start with that?

Because she was being a chicken. Things between them felt fragile and new, one breath away from tipping one way or the other. Another few weeks and they'd be head over boots in love, settled into a pattern.

Or maybe she was the only one falling all over again, thoughts about the future starting to whisper at her.

Sadie bit her thumbnail. "And of course it's not just about the ranch. You and I…" Her heart beat against her rib cage. "I've had such an amazing time this past week."

"Yeah, it's been nice." He grabbed his clothes and started pulling them on, his movements quick and precise, his attention focused on the motion. "Don't worry about the ranch. We'll be fine."

She quickly dressed and then stood up and caught his arm. "Royce. Wait. We need to talk about this."

He sighed, put both of his hands on her shoulders, and kissed her, one soft press of his lips. "There's nothing to talk about. It's a second chance with your music, just like we were discussing earlier. You've got to go."

He snuffed out the fire, gathered the equipment, and untied the horses. Then he got onto Thor. Sadie wanted to tell him to slow down and give her a damn minute to try to figure out everything, but she didn't have it figured out, and she wasn't sure that she could say she didn't have to leave.

Shit, shit, shit.

When they got back to the barn, they unsaddled the horses and put them in their stalls. Royce checked in on Chevy and Shadow as Sadie watched on. He moved to put away the bridles, and Chevy hung her head over the stall, begging for her head to be rubbed with a soft neigh. Sadie ran her hand down the mama horse's nose and watched as her filly wobbled around between her legs. They felt like her horses, too, and suddenly she couldn't imagine leaving them right now. Chevy was still recovering, and what if the baby needed extra attention?

And what about Duke? She glanced back at his stall. One ride wasn't enough for them to get to know each other the way she'd planned.

Then there was Royce... Yearning and worry pressed against her lungs as she watched him move around the barn, now onto positioning the saddles just so.

If she left, who was going to remind him to slow down and take a break once in a while? To get into water fights, sing in the truck, and race on horseback to the river?

Everything was happening too fast, and panic over making the wrong decision filled her up until it was impossible to breathe.

Finally, Royce turned around and she placed herself in

front of him so he couldn't ignore her anymore.

"Royce."

He stared down at her, his expression unreadable.

She wrapped her arms around his waist and hugged him. For a moment it was like hugging a log, but then he gave in and hugged her back. His clothes were cool from being outside, he smelled like grass and cologne, and as she listened to his heart beating under her ear, she couldn't imagine ever letting go. "Maybe...maybe I should just say no. It's not really a good time for me to leave."

"For what? To stay here?" He shook his head and laughed, a hollow sound that made pain radiate through her chest. "Sadie, we agreed this was just a fun thing while you were here. I guess I should've made it clearer before, but... I'm not looking for a serious relationship." He turned and rattled the gate like he was checking to see if it was latched and then glanced at her. "So don't be stupid — you'd be crazy to turn down an opportunity like that."

If she could talk past the lump rising in her throat, she'd tell him that she wasn't stupid.

Apparently she was just unrealistically optimistic. Maybe that was the same thing as being stupid, though. She'd thought he'd felt the same. That they were both falling together. All this time she worried she'd accidentally hurt him again, and he was the one breaking her heart. But he was also right. What was she going to do? Turn down a contract opportunity with Belle Meade? To work on a horse ranch with a guy she could never fully have?

"Morning will be here too soon, and I've got a lot on my plate tomorrow. I better turn in." Royce reached out like he was going to put his hand on her back, and then quickly dropped it. "I'll walk you to your truck."

Their footsteps against the hard dirt of the driveway sounded so loud in the quiet.

Were they really going to leave things like this?

"Aren't we at least friends anymore?" she asked, her voice just above a whisper.

Royce reached over her and opened the truck door. "Of course. We'll always be friends. So you can, you know, call or whatever to tell me how the meeting goes if you want to. Or I guess I'll hear it through the town grapevine."

She wanted to scream that friends didn't learn things about each other through the stupid-ass town grapevine!

Sheer force of will was all that was holding back the tears. "I'll be back for the rodeo, so I can tell you myself—I already committed to singing, and then I can say good-bye to the kids before they all return to their homes."

"I'm sure the kids and the town would understand if you canceled."

"Well, I wouldn't be okay with that. *I've* gotten too attached."

The way he was staring at the ground, the brim of his hat covering his eyes, made it impossible to tell if he'd even had a reaction to that.

"So I'll see you at the rodeo," she said. "And if I don't get a chance to tell you before your events, good luck."

"Yeah, you, too. With the singing."

A tear slipped down her cheek—so much for her force of will. She leaned in and kissed his lips, a quick peck that was nowhere near worthy of being a good-bye kiss.

But Royce certainly didn't bother making it anything more.

Chapter Fifteen

"Addison. Eli." Royce had given the rest of the kids their instructions and sent them on their way. At the sound of their names, they flinched—he also noticed they'd been holding hands, but quickly let go. "You've got five days to prove to me that I can trust you. If you work hard and there are no more incidents, you can go to the rodeo."

"Really?" Addison squealed, and Royce smiled despite himself.

At the feel of a hand on his arm, he turned to find Mom beaming at him. Apparently she approved.

"Make me regret it, and I'll take it away in an instant. Don't think I won't."

Eli looked around. "Where's Sadie? She's the one who talked you into the rodeo, isn't she?"

Her name sent stabbing pain through Royce. Working to keep his face neutral, he nodded. "Now, go get to work so you'll be done in time to ride to the river."

"Yes, sir," Eli said, not even an ounce of sarcasm in the words. He grabbed Addison's hand, and Royce was about to say something about it, but he let it go. He just didn't have the energy to get on them for a relatively innocent gesture.

"Where *is* Sadie?" Mom asked, glancing toward the empty spot her truck usually occupied.

"Gone."

Mom's eyebrows drew together. "Gone?"

Royce clenched his jaw and breathed out his nose, trying to counteract the way his chest tightened. Their conversation last night about her leaving had left him raw and exhausted in ways that sleep couldn't fix. He'd been sure Sadie was going to see through him—see how much he was tempted to beg her to stay. Every time she talked about music, though, he saw it—she wasn't going to be happy giving up on it. It'd been there in her voice last night, and he'd seen the longing on her face during that phone call. So he'd forced away thoughts of the future he dreamed of having with her and pushed her as hard as he could, not wanting to be a decision she later regretted. She'd had to go and draw out the good-bye, making it so damn hard to hold back his emotions. That tear that'd run down her cheek at the end had nearly killed him, and watching her drive away had made him ache in muscles he didn't even realize he had.

Then he'd walked into his empty, empty house, thinking how her laughter would never bounce off the walls again. How there'd be no late-night chocolate milk or hours spent in his bed, both awake and asleep.

Misery ebbed in and out with every beat of his heart. *How the hell did I let this happen again?*

Mom waved a hand in front of his face. "Hey. Are you

purposely being vague to drive me crazy? I thought you two were...well, it looked like you were together again. You both seemed so happy."

He worked to keep his voice even. "She told me she couldn't promise she'd stay." *I should've seen it then. Should've put a stop to everything before it turned into this.* "She's flying back to Nashville today. Has some big meeting with record execs tomorrow, and, unless they're deaf and blind, I have no doubt she'll have a recording contract within a few days. So, I'll see about hiring someone else before the next group of kids comes in, but you, Cory, and I will be stretched thin this week. Sorry about that."

He turned to go, nearly tripping over Oscar, which earned him a hiss.

"You let her go?" Mom said from behind him, and the spot between his shoulder blades tightened.

He slowly spun around. "*Let* her? Mom, I can't compete with a record contract. And this land, my horses, even the camp..." Until he'd mentioned the camp, he didn't realize how much it meant to him. Probably because Sadie's being here had allowed him to relax long enough to see the changes in the kids instead of just the stress of running the place. The alternative camp had been his dad's legacy, but it was his now. He put a hand on his chest. "It's everything I am. I'd never leave it behind, and that means I could never make her happy. She's destined for bigger things."

"Did you at least tell her how you feel?"

Clearly, Mom could see that he'd fallen back in love with Sadie. He hadn't dared to even think it, but the knowledge that he did love her washed over him, shoving the ache deep into his bones. And he found himself opening his mouth to admit the thing he'd never told anyone. Not Cory. Not Dad. He'd expected people in town to find out, but Sadie must not have admitted it either—well, except to Quinn. He had no doubt Sadie had told her what'd happened. He'd proposed. Like the lovesick fool that he was. "I asked her to marry me."

Shock flickered across Mom's face. "You asked her to marry you? When? Last night?"

"Six years ago." He remembered the silence in the truck after he'd asked her. He hadn't really planned it—didn't even have a ring. He'd just looked across the cab and known she was the one. So he'd asked her to marry him. She'd started to cry, and he'd instinctually known that they weren't tears of joy. "She took off for Nashville right after. I'm not going to be the schmuck who gets left for that place twice."

Mom's mouth opened and closed a few times before she got any words out. "I didn't know." She hugged him, and he sighed. Now she was upset, too, and treating him like he was a little kid who needed consoling.

"I'm fine, Mom. It was a long time ago." *And I'd be over it if I hadn't gone and reopened the wound so it'd have to heal all over again.* He gently patted her back. "Now I've got to get back to work."

At least today would be busy with rodeo prep and the ride to the river. Saddles would need to be checked, and he still had to gather all of the fishing gear. Of course, when he got to the barn and saw Shadow, he realized it didn't matter how busy he was. He'd still see Sadie every place he looked.

• • •

Sadie's entire family had decided they were dropping her off at the airport, and from the grim looks on everyone's faces, you'd think she was going to a funeral, not on her way to the biggest opportunity of her life.

I've got to be careful. Building it up too much will just make it worse if it doesn't work out. And that was what she wanted. For it to work out.

It should be what she wanted, anyway.

Sadie hugged Grandma first.

"Don't forget about us once you're a big fancy star," she said with a smile.

Tears pushed in on Sadie's eyes, and suddenly everything seemed so final that the grim expressions made sense. Even though she was planning on coming back, she knew the next few years might be a whirlwind, and she worried about not being there for her family. She'd never even learned how to make rolls the right, non-lumpy way. Or the amazing fudge frosting for the brownies.

Not that she thought she'd have a lot of time to bake. Or that she could eat any of those things anymore. Her smallest jeans no longer fit, and even the next size up was getting snug.

The smile on her face was hard to hold onto as she turned to Mom. "I thought we'd have all this time, and now it's gone," Mom said, wrapping her arms around Sadie. "I should've known it'd only be a matter of time before someone saw you were as amazing as I know you are."

"Let's not get ahead of ourselves. It's just one meeting, I'll only be gone for a few days, and then we'll take it from there, depending on what happens." Sadie said it for her benefit as much as Mom's. "Either way, I promise to visit more. This isn't our last opportunity to talk. Okay?"

Mom started to pull away, but then she hesitated. "I know I don't say it enough, but I'm so proud of you. Most people would've given up, but you just keep brushing yourself off and hitting it again. I don't know if I could've done it."

Sadie nodded, her throat too tight to talk.

"But you know I'll be proud no matter what happens, right?" Mom ran her hand down Sadie's hair. "I never wanted you to make my mistakes, but I'm afraid that somewhere along the way, I gave you the impression I'd only be proud of you if you became a big star or made a lot of money. For all my griping and complaining, I'm happy with how my life turned out. I've got my parents, I've got you, and while my job's exhausting, I like what I do. The real secret's finding joy in whatever path you end up on. Whichever one you take, I'll always be on your side, and I'll support you however I can." Mom squeezed her hand. "I love you, Sadie."

Her heart expanded and constricted all at once. She'd needed to hear that so badly right now, yet it made it that much harder to say good-bye. "Love you, too, Mom."

She pulled her in for another motherly hug. "Now you be sure to call once you land, and keep us updated on the meeting, okay?"

Sadie nodded, blinking and taking deep breaths to try to fight the urge to cry.

Grandpa stepped up for his good-bye last, and then no amount of blinking or breathing held the tears at bay. She hugged him with every ounce of strength she had in her. Now she was thinking about Mom's talk of paths, and she was only more confused. "I'd be crazy to turn down this opportunity, right?"

"Oh, don't ask me. I'm just an old horse rancher who's

never even been on an airplane and has no desire to live around so many people. But your voice would sure sound pretty on the radio. I know that much." He pulled back and squeezed her shoulder. "You need me to carry your luggage inside?"

She sniffed and wiped the tears from her cheeks. "No, they'll get mad at you if you leave your car." A quick tug on the handle of her suitcase extended it to hip height. "I can just roll it, anyway."

She glanced off in the distance, at the blue mountains set against a clear sunny sky. For some reason, all she could see was Royce. This was where he belonged, and this past month, she'd started to think she might, too.

Just having fun. That was all we were doing. If things were different, if he wanted more... But that was a dangerous line of thought, one she couldn't indulge in without getting hurt—and her heart already ached so badly she wasn't sure it'd ever recover. So Sadie took her last breath of Wyoming air for a while and headed into the airport.

Hopefully on her way to all of her dreams coming true.

Chapter Sixteen

"What did you do to your hair?" Nolan asked the second Sadie met him outside the studio Saturday morning. His scowl deepened as he lifted a section and tugged it closer to his face. Once he released her hair, his gaze moved to her stomach. "Looks like someone's let her exercise and diet slide."

Actually, she'd been working her ass off on the ranch. Yes, she'd put on a little weight, but she'd also gained muscle—a more athletic than skinny body. Not that Nolan would believe her. She ran a hand through her hair. "It's fresh. Different." *Me.*

"The execs don't want different. They want tried and true." He opened the door and ushered her inside like the gentleman he wasn't. When she'd first looked for an agent, she had visions of someone who'd love her voice and get her and be, like, a music cheerleader. She'd quickly learned that wasn't how it was. While Nolan was known for being a shark when it came to negotiations and getting his clients the best deals, he also did that whole I'm-making-you-better-by-pointing-out-your-flaws-so-we-can-fix-you thing.

Despite his telling her she'd need a thick skin to be in this biz, and the pep talks she'd given herself reiterating the same thing, his words always stung. Over the years, she'd gotten accustomed to it, but after feeling pretty good about herself and being away from it all, she was surprised at how much it ate at her now.

Biting back a comment about *his* gut, she forced a smile on her face and focused on what was important—singing her best and impressing the record exec.

She met Linda Call, who told her how much she'd enjoyed hearing her sing in Louisiana, which was like a balm to her singer's soul and helped her remember why she was doing this in the first place. She loved singing onstage—loved the music and the energy of the crowd and that moment when she connected to them and they connected to her.

After a few more minutes of polite small talk, she was ushered into the studio. Of course her brain chose that moment to relive her last awful performance onstage. Panic rose up as she stared at the large microphone, and her throat went bone-dry.

Think of something else. She reached for a good singing experience and came up with the night she'd sung around the campfire. When she lingered on the memory, she started thinking of the faces glowing in the firelight—faces she missed so badly a pang went through her chest—so she redirected her thoughts to the pureness of music sung that way. To how big her voice had felt in all that open space.

Then she went bigger scale, back to the buzz of the

audience in Louisiana and nailing the cover she'd been given to sing, and how that had led her to this moment right now. This awesome opportunity that she needed to take hold of and use to show that she deserved to be here.

I can do this, I can do this. She stepped closer to the microphone and nodded to show she was ready, then took a deep breath to center herself. The song she usually liked to start with was Carrie Underwood's "Do You Think About Me."

The music started up, and despite her trembling hands, she hit the first notes—with less volume than usual, but the sound was pure. She closed her eyes, trying to focus on letting the song flow out of her. Only as she sang the lyrics, she found herself near tears. Royce clearly didn't think about her the way she thought about him, but she knew he had to feel something. They had history. Sure, there were some bad memories mixed in there, but most of them were good.

Apparently, good wasn't good enough.

Nolan and Linda stared at her through the thick glass between them, and neither looked impressed, which only made her voice shakier. Made the tears press down harder.

"I'm sorry," she said as she finished. "I just need a quick water break, if that's okay."

A wide-eyed girl who had to be fresh out of high school brought in bottled water. Sadie imagined it was what she'd looked like when she'd first come to Nashville, dreams shining in her eyes. It sucked that each year had jaded her more and more.

Shake it off. No more living in the past. This is your future, so grab hold of it and show it who's boss. By the time she stepped up to the microphone again, she was ready.

No more nerves or shakiness or thinking about Royce. For the better part of the morning, she went from one song to another, taking requests as Linda or Nolan threw them at her, and she managed to get a few smiles and nods out of them as well.

By the time she and Nolan settled across the desk from Linda, she felt like she'd at least given it her best.

I just hope it's good enough.

"Don't worry," Nolan said, scooting forward in his seat. "She'll lose ten pounds by the end of the month, and she's just between hair extensions. Usually it's platinum blond."

Linda looked her over. "You know, she might be able to pull off red. I'm thinking lots of volume with extensions. Bright red, super-sexy image. With your face, and after some hard work on your body, we can do a provocative photo shoot and get some buzz going. Make the guys stop and drool a little, you know?"

Of course she wanted to look sexy, but where was the sexy line? Did that mean her needed-to-be enhanced cleavage hanging out? Half naked? She thought of all the people in Hope Springs looking at the photos and then covering up their kids' eyes. *What about Mom, Grandpa, and Grandma?* She'd always hated how girls had to be straddling guitars or shot with bedroom hair for CD covers while guys got to go with simple and fully clothed.

If the deal goes through, I'll let them know I have lines I don't want to cross.

Linda sat back in her chair. "I'm also thinking a little less twang. We want to appeal to the largest audience, both country and pop fans."

Sadie must've wrinkled her nose, because Linda gave

her a placating smile. "Once we get you established, you'll have a little more wiggle room on the look and songs. I hate it as much as you do, but singers are a dime a dozen, and despite what the American people say, they care about weight and looks as much as they do the music. Stick with me, and I'll make you a star."

Linda obviously had the ambition, which meant she'd work like crazy to get Sadie on the radio. If she was going to work hard enough to stay ten pounds lighter and hold back the twang that tended to come out when she really let loose, she wanted someone who'd be working hard, too. And Sadie wasn't totally opposed to red hair—she could make it work, she supposed. Quinn would probably go crazy over the bright hue.

Red hair. Less country. Ten pounds off, so no more bread or pastries.

Funny enough, as she was sitting there, it wasn't a country song that popped into her head. It was Pink, singing about how she'd be a pop star. All she'd have to change was everything she was.

The image of Royce staring down at her, desire in his eyes, suddenly came to mind. Then she heard his voice. *You were perfect the way you were. The way you are now.*

Of course, he had been staring down at her in his too-large shirt, and they'd been about to have sex.

A toxic mix of longing and regret burned through her, and she shook her head, telling herself to snap out of it. *A hundred women would line up to take my place right now. I won't make the mistake my former bandmates made. I can deal.*

Linda and Nolan were going over a few stipulations,

things she knew she should pay better attention to, but which went in one ear and out the other.

"So, let's talk contract," Nolan said, and Linda leaned her elbows on her desk and steepled her fingers under her chin.

"Let's."

Nolan grinned, and Sadie wondered why she had to work so hard to do the same.

• • •

Sadie paused near the display of chocolate muffins in the airport coffee shop and then passed them by with a sigh. She'd only been on her stupid diet for three days, but the sight of pastries made her slightly bitter at life, and the heavenly scents of French fries and pizza filling the air weren't helping, either.

I'll just ask Quinn to pull over somewhere I can get a good salad before we head out of town. If she tried to order a salad in Hope Springs that wasn't just a side for steak or fried chicken, people would stare at her as if she were on the verge of lunacy. Sheila at the diner would probably even put a hand to her forehead and ask if she was feeling all right. *I'm gonna have to try to stay away from Grandma's amazing cooking, too, or I'll undo the past few days.*

Sadie had spent most of Sunday and Monday looking at apartments and filling out applications. Having so much to do had been good, because whenever she'd slow down, sadness would creep in, and she'd spent last night in her hotel room crying herself to sleep. "Weepy mess" was the best way to describe her lately, and she hated it. It was ridiculous, but no matter how much she told herself to stop, her emotions refused to listen. She knew it was just the transition period and the past month catching up to her. It'd happened the first time she'd moved to Nashville, and eventually she'd gotten over it, so she'd get over it again.

After a ten-minute wait at the baggage claim, she gathered her suitcase and texted Quinn that she was heading outside.

A silver Mercedes coupe pulled up in front of Sadie, and she was going to frown at the driver for blocking Quinn's way, but then she realized it *was* Quinn.

Sadie met her at the back of the car. "Holy crap, girl! Did you boost a car on your way here?"

"Figured it was the fastest way to get us to Hope Springs," Quinn said with a grin. "You like it? Daddy said I needed a new car to impress clients, and who am I to argue? The company's even paying for it." She bumped her hip into Sadie. "So, how's life now that you're on your way to being super famous?"

Sadie heaved her suitcase into the trunk. "I can't wait until I can make odd diva demands. Like no brown M&M's. Who wants to eat boring-colored candy?"

They got into the car, and Quinn said, "And you should get that, like, super-snooty water and demand exotic flowers for your dressing rooms."

"But I'll always keep my fans in mind and do big signings for them, because I'll never forget they're what's really important."

"Of course." Quinn glanced over her shoulder and then hit the gas pedal, shooting them into traffic. "I'm so proud of you—I always knew it'd happen."

"Thanks."

"Uh-oh." Quinn glanced at her. "Thanks? Not, 'OMG, I'm so happy I'm gonna start singing and dancing and there's gonna be fireworks later'?"

Sadie glanced at the ceiling, swearing under her breath. How could more tears be trying to come out?

"Spill it."

"All I can think about is Royce. His stupid handsome face and the ranch and the horses and the way he makes me feel." Sadie leaned forward and placed her forehead on the dashboard. She sniffed and then said, "In case you were wondering, even the dashboard of this thing is comfy."

"Great, because I hope I have lots of clients who feel the need to fling themselves on it." Quinn put her hand on Sadie's back. "I hate to state the obvious here, but I think you should talk to Royce. You're clearly in love with him."

"Yeah, but I was in love with him in high school, too, and in the end, it didn't matter." The familiar ache dug its claws into her chest, gripping her heart tighter. "We want different things—I even tried to tell him how I feel, that maybe I could stay, and he told me that he was only on board to have fun for a while. That he wasn't interested in a serious relationship. I think I broke him. Broke us." She wiped at a tear that ran down her face. "It's really over."

"I'm sorry, babe."

Sadie popped up so fast she knocked into Quinn's outstretched arm. "And it's so frustrating, because I should be happy! There *should* be fireworks! I think it just hasn't hit me yet that the recording contract's real. We went over all the ins and outs, and Nolan called me this morning to say they'd emailed it to him. He wanted to go over it, and then he'll overnight it to me to sign." She nodded. "It'll feel real then. I'll be more excited, I swear."

Sadie bit her lip. "Except for, you know, I can't stop asking myself if I really want to dye my hair red and deal with extensions again and be on a diet for the rest of my life. Or tone down what's actually unique about my voice and live so far away from all my family and friends. But I'll be on the road a lot if it goes well, anyway, so…"

"Well, do you?" Quinn glanced at her. "Do you want those things?"

"A thousand people would take my spot right now."

"That's not a real answer."

"You sound just like your dad."

Quinn gasped and shoved her, and despite Sadie's gloomy mood, she laughed. Then she looked at her best friend and the damn waterworks started all over again. "I think my dream changed somewhere along the way. I do want to sing, I just don't know in what capacity anymore. I don't know if I can give up this opportunity and live with myself, though—I know I can't give it up for a maybe."

They still had a half an hour left in their drive, and Sadie didn't want to think about those things anymore—she knew the rodeo tomorrow night would be hard enough as it was. "Time for a subject change. Tell me something interesting."

Quinn told off a driver who'd cut in front of her only to slow down, and then went around the car. "Okay, subject change… Oh, I know! Guess what I just found out? The Mountain Ridge Bed and Breakfast might be going up for sale."

"Yeah, I heard that."

Quinn whipped her head toward Sadie. "And you didn't

tell me?"

"Well, I thought a deal for someone else to buy it was already in the works."

"So? Do you know what I do for a living? I destroy other deals so that I can get the properties I want, and I've wanted that property since I was a little girl. I've already instructed the town committee to let me know when it's going on the market."

"Then what? You're going to update it and run a B and B?"

The corner of Quinn's mouth lifted, and she got that glint in her eye that meant she was starting to calculate a plan. "Yes. And it's gonna be the best damn B and B ever."

Chapter Seventeen

Trying to get everyone ready for the rodeo was pretty much organized madness, and it made Royce question if it was a good idea all over again. Mom's friend Sheila had come over with her van to help transport the teens, and she and Mom reassured him the kids were good and that they could handle them.

Still, Royce worried one of the teens would leave the stands under the pretense of getting a snow cone or going to the bathroom and end up sneaking off—or worse, a pair of them would disappear together. There was trust, and then there was realizing they were teenagers.

Chevy whickered at him as he walked by with Thor, and he paused to pat her head. "You know I'd take you with me normally." He glanced at the big black quarter horse by his side. "No offense, Thor."

Shadow bounced over to Chevy and darted around her mother's legs. Because his mind was determined to torture him lately, it chose to flash back to the night he and Sadie spent down in the straw, delivering the foal. If Sadie hadn't driven over, he wondered if he would've been able to calm Chevy down by himself. He doubted it.

Without her at the ranch the past few days, work was piling up again, threatening to crush him. Finding a replacement who was as well equipped to handle both the horses and the kids was going to be impossible. He knew all too well there was no such thing as replacing Sadie Hart. And now he was going to have to face her one last time before she took off again.

He sucked in a deep breath and then loaded Thor into the trailer and double-checked that he had all of his roping gear.

"You ready?" Cory asked as they climbed into the cab of the truck.

I probably should've prepared for the bronc riding better. Hold on. That was the most important part. He could fudge the rest. "Ready as I'll ever be. It's just a small-town rodeo anyway, right?"

"Yeah, if you leave out the part where your ex-girlfriend is singing the national anthem and the entire population of that small town will be looking on to see what's going on between you two."

The engine growled to life as Royce turned the key. "Thanks for that."

"No problem," Cory said with a grin.

As he drove toward the rodeo grounds, though, Royce knew he wasn't ready to see Sadie again. That he'd never be, even if it was also the thing he craved more than anything in the world.

. . .

"What does a panic attack feel like?" Sadie called down the stairs. "Because I'm pretty sure I'm having one."

Quinn was at the bottom talking to Grandpa, most likely about the weather or the big city or who knew what? Sadie was too busy having a panic attack.

"I'll talk to you later, Mr. Manning," Quinn said, flashing Grandpa a grin before rushing up the stairs.

Sadie waved a hand in front of her face, hoping cool air would help. "My heart is racing and I can't breathe and my skin is too big and too small at the same time."

Quinn placed her hands on Sadie's shoulders. "Which thing are we panicking about? Singing at the rodeo? Seeing Royce? The contract that came FedEx this afternoon?"

Sadie's hummingbird heartbeat kicked it up a notch. "Yes. But I figure I should focus on deciding what to wear first. I ain't singing the national anthem in my yoga pants."

Nearly every piece of clothing she owned was on her bed. Her skinny jeans reminded her that she'd gained weight she needed to lose, but she had plenty of other nice jeans with varying designs on the pockets, everything from swirls to fleurs-de-lis to flowers—all with rhinestones, of course. But then she decided maybe she should wear a skirt or dress, and then she'd picked up the pen to sign her contract, and then her pulse had hammered through her head, so she'd gone back to the pile of clothes, only to decide she had nothing to wear.

Quinn picked up a pair of super-short fringed shorts and raised an eyebrow.

"Those are from high school. I pulled them out when I thought I might have something better in my old clothes. I didn't."

The shorts got tossed off to the side.

"I'm actually nervous to sing, too, for some reason. I mean, I've sung in front of large audiences before. I have a singing contract waiting for me to sign. Why am I suddenly sure I'm going to choke again? Or forget the words?" Sadie started running them over in her head.

"Hey, if Christina Aguilera can do it and survive, so can you." Quinn turned and then her smile dropped. "That was supposed to cheer you up, not make you look like you've seen a ghost."

Sadie nodded. "Oh. Right." Her head just kept on nodding, like it forgot how to stop.

"Going in and out of the arena in a skirt might get tricky, so…" Quinn tapped a finger to her lips. "Casual but sexy." She grabbed a pair of distressed denim jeans with silver thread and rhinestones on the pockets. "About to be famous." Her hand skimmed along the tops, and then she picked out the coral sleeveless one with cream lace and beading along the neckline. "With a side of *eat your heart out, stupid idiot who doesn't want a relationship.*"

Quinn thrust it all at her. "Add your boots with the flowers and a nice big belt…" She dug through the pile and came out with one. "Now, get dressed. You're going to rock this, and you're gonna look super hot doing it."

A little more than thirty minutes later, Sadie, Quinn, Grandma, Grandpa, and Mom were seated in a prime spot in the grandstands, up front where Sadie could easily get out when it was time for her to sing. Her foot took on a life of its own, tapping faster and faster the more people arrived. When Sadie spotted Caroline, Sheila, and the kids from Second Chance Ranch toward the top of the bleachers in the next section over, she excused herself to go say hello.

Eli waved as she approached. "Sadie! Hey!" He stood and grinned as she made her way up the last few bleachers. She wasn't sure if they were supposed to refrain from hugging the kids, but she figured she didn't work there anymore, so it didn't matter. She squeezed Eli tightly, surprised at how much she hated the thought of never seeing him again. Or any of the rest of the kids, for that matter.

So she hugged them all, and then turned to Caroline, who didn't waste any time pulling Sadie into her arms. "It's good to see you, hon. We all missed you." Caroline drew back and looked Sadie in the eye. "All of us. Even if one of us refuses to say it."

I'm not gonna cry, I'm not gonna cry. "I missed you all, too."

"So…how'd the—was it an audition—go?"

"It went really well. They want me to sign a contract and record an album!" The enthusiasm shouldn't have been so hard to fake, but bless Caroline, she congratulated her with a big smile on her face. She'd claimed Royce missed her, too, but, even if it were true, Sadie needed more than missing.

I need him to love me the way I love him.

Sadie's phone rang, and she stepped away to take the call.

"We need you down here now," Patsy Higgins said. "Are you ready to sing?"

Sadie nodded and then realized Patsy couldn't see her—well, since she was setting up the microphone at the front of the area and Sadie could see her, it might be possible, but the nodding was probably hard to make out. "I'll be right there."

• • •

The horses were ready. The gear was good to go. Royce and Cory were signed in and had their numbers pinned on. Everything was set. The bleachers and grandstands were full, most of the people from Hope Springs there, as well as plenty of others from nearby towns, here to compete and watch.

Even though Royce hadn't done any competing since last year's Fourth of July rodeo, he wasn't nervous—not about the roping or riding, anyway. As Sadie walked to the middle of the arena, though, microphone in hand, nerves jumped around in his gut, and his heart beat like it meant to come right out of his chest.

Her hair was curled in big waves that framed her pretty face, she had on a bright-colored top that shimmered in the sunlight along with the big sparkly earrings she wore, and she had on blessedly tight rhinestoned jeans.

Earlier, when Patsy Higgins had passed by, he'd heard her going on and on about how Sadie had a big music contract now, and proudly declaring she'd always known it'd happen. He'd known it, too, but it didn't stop his heart from sinking as the hope he thought he'd already snuffed out completely disappeared.

"Hi, everybody," Sadie said into the microphone, flashing the audience a giant grin as she waved. "It's been so long since I've been to a rodeo, and I'm crazy excited to get started. Are y'all ready for this?"

The crowd erupted in applause, shouts, and whistles, and Sadie's grin widened.

She shone out there in the spotlight. Once again, it hit him that he had to let her go. He knew—through experience—that he could survive it. Which was how he knew that without her in his life, it'd always be a little less colorful, slightly boring… The spot between his ribs ached. A lot more empty.

Sometimes he wished he didn't know that, but as he watched her take the centering moment she always did before she started a song, he decided that he didn't regret having had another chance to be around her. Or the amazing nights they'd had together.

The microphone neared her full lips—lips covered in a shade of lipstick that nearly matched her shirt—and then she started singing the anthem. Just her, that amazing voice, the spellbound audience, and the energy crackling through the air.

He pushed the hand he had over his heart a little harder, wishing it'd stop the longing pumping through it. As soon as she finished, he decided that he'd say something when she passed by to go back to the grandstands. They needed a real good-bye, and he wanted to tell her congratulations on her singing career taking off, even if it'd kill him a little to say it aloud because it made it that much more real.

The sound of clanging metal and a neigh mixed with swearing and yelling caught his attention. A horse was rearing up, and one of the other contestants—a teenage boy—was struggling to get control of the horse. Royce ducked though the fence separating them and caught the reins of the animal, talking calmly with a hand on its neck until it settled down.

"You okay?" Royce asked, and the cowboy nodded, red creeping into his face. "It's okay. Happens to the best of us from time to time."

"Thanks," the kid said.

Royce nodded and turned, his thoughts on Sadie.

Only she'd already passed by and was heading up the bleachers to sit with her family.

. . .

"You did great!" Grandma said, hugging Sadie. Grandpa patted her shoulder and Mom squeezed her hand.

Quinn slung her arm over Sadie's shoulders as she settled into her seat. "When you're big and famous, I'm going to constantly tell everyone I'm your best friend. Like, perfect strangers will just be walking by, and I'll stop them to tell them."

Sadie forced her lips into a smile, and Quinn raised an eyebrow, clearly seeing through it. "It's okay," Sadie said. "I just wanna enjoy the rodeo. But tonight I want you to come over while I pack, and I need you to bring the strongest alcohol you can get your hands on."

Quinn nodded but hugged her a little tighter. When Sadie had seen Royce standing near the exit, all decked out in a dressy black hat, blue-and-black plaid shirt, and chaps, longing had filled every inch of her body. She'd anticipated walking by and at least saying hi and good luck. She desperately needed some kind of closure, even though she knew that wasn't really possible when it came to her and

Royce.

But he'd left as soon as she headed toward him. Which was either anger or a level of indifference she couldn't bear thinking of. Every inch of her ached, and she couldn't wait until tonight when she could numb herself from it all for a while. She didn't want to think about how bad the following days would be, or how long it'd take to stop crying every time she thought of him.

When the steer roping started, she sat up a little straighter. Despite Royce's explanation about why they did the event, she still cheered for most of the cows to get away — or at least take a while to be caught, so Royce would have extra seconds to work with. She noticed things she'd never noticed before, like the way the horse immediately pulled back when the steer was roped — and the ones who didn't. How fast they burst out of the gate. The disqualifiers, from the horse breaking the barrier or the ropes being kicked loose. She could call it before it came over the loud speakers.

Then the announcer said Royce's name. It hung in the air as her vision tunneled to the spot where he was setting up. At his signal, a black steer shot into the arena, and then Royce and Thor came barreling out after it. A couple swings from the lasso and then Royce launched the rope, catching the cow's head. In one smooth movement he was off Thor, flipping the cow and binding its feet. He threw up his hands and Sadie stared at the scoreboard. They waited the extra time to ensure he'd tied it tight enough it couldn't kick loose, and when Royce's steer remained bound, the red numbers lit up.

Nine point two seconds.

The audience erupted in cheers. All of the other

contenders had been in the fourteen- to twenty-second range. They did another round, and by the end, no surprise, Royce was the winner. As he sat perched on top of one of the gates and waved to the crowd, Sadie suddenly got this image of him next to Chevy and Shadow with a little cowboy who looked like him and a little cowgirl who looked like her by his side. She closed her eyes and fell into the image, putting herself next to them and the horses. Kissing Royce as their kids ran around the yard of the ranch.

The feeling that washed over her was the same one she used to get when she thought of herself onstage in a sold-out arena, preparing to sing one of the hits from her debut album.

Sadie quickly opened her eyes and focused on the clown in the middle of the arena, who was now making jokes with the announcer to pass a few minutes between events. *Stupid imagination.*

Steer wrestling was up next, and when Cory's turn came around, she and Quinn cheered like crazy for him. After he won, they high-fived like they'd been personally responsible. They repeated cheering and high-fiving when he and Royce took first in the team roping contest—the boys were really cleaning up today.

After a few more events, it was time for bronc riding. Just like in high school, she regretted everything she'd eaten, and she couldn't stop rubbing her palms up and down her jeans. "I hate this part."

Quinn watched the horse bucking wildly as the cowboy tried to hang on. "Hey, I hate to admit it, but it's totally hot. Makes me want a cowboy."

Sadie tried to swallow past the lump of anxiety that'd

lodged in her throat. "It's different when it is your cowboy." A sharp pain clenched her chest. "Not that I have one."

"Oh, you have one. And he's up next."

The pickup men herded the now riderless bucking bronco toward the gate, and the guys manning it swung it open to let it through. When the previous rider was out of the area, Royce set up on the horse he'd drawn—Nacho Man. If a horse was named that, Sadie didn't want to think about how crazy that meant it was.

She grabbed Quinn's hand as the loud buzz pierced the air. The horse shot out like it meant to fly to the moon, and Royce clung on, one of his hands waving through the air. Each second took an eternity, and Sadie could feel her blood pressure steadily rising.

Just hold on for a little longer, babe.

And don't get crushed, okay? My heart couldn't take it.

The eight-second buzz sounded out and Sadie released a shaky breath. There was still the dismount to worry about, though. The horse got in front of the pickup men and Royce bailed off, sending up a cloud of dust but landing on his feet.

Just when relief was starting to wind through her, the horse charged him, still bucking like mad.

"Oh holy shit!" Sadie was on her feet before she realized she was going to stand. Royce jumped out of the way, clinging to the nearby fence, and the horse bolted past him and out of the arena. She threw her hands over her rapidly beating heart and took a few deep breaths, trying to get the adrenaline coursing through her body to calm down.

The entire crowd was looking at her now. She let out a nervous laugh to try to show she was perfectly fine and then plopped back down next to Quinn. Maybe it was only her paranoid imagination, but it seemed like everyone started whispering about her.

The announcer was asking Royce a couple of questions, so he was still in the area, his Wranglers and chaps coated in dust.

And all she saw was the guy she'd never have.

The life she'd never have.

Agony gripped her body, holding each muscle prisoner. "I need to go." Sadie couldn't even tell her family good-bye, because then the entire town would see her burst into tears. She'd sign that contract, pack up, and then she'd put all of this behind her. She'd work so hard that her grief would have no choice but to take a backseat. In the quiet moments, when it caught up to her and tried to drag her down…well, she wasn't sure how she'd get through it, but if she thought about that now, she'd drop down to the ground and never be able to get up again.

"…the microphone?" the announcer asked in the background.

"Wait up, Sadie." Quinn's footsteps followed behind her. "I'm coming."

Sadie pounded down the steps of the grandstand and hit the ground, starting to round to the walkway that'd take her out to the parking lot.

"Sadie Hart."

She froze at the sound of Royce's voice. Slowly turned around to see him standing in the middle of the arena.

"You best not be leaving yet, because I have something I need to say."

Chapter Eighteen

Royce had thought that hiring Sadie had been the dumbest decision he'd ever made, but he was about to top it.

After he'd jumped off that bucking bronco, all he could think was that he didn't want it to be the last exciting thing he ever did. Sadie was a risk, like those eight seconds of wondering if you were going to be able to hold on. There was a good chance of being dumped on your ass, but man, was the in-between time amazing.

Then suddenly he'd looked up and seen her leaving, and he'd panicked and asked for the microphone that he was now clutching so hard he was surprised it didn't crack. The girl had rejected him before, and he couldn't help thinking she was about to do it again, but this time, it'd be in front of everyone.

Yet, he couldn't stop. Couldn't hold it back anymore.

Trying to block out all the faces staring at him except for one, he said. "I lied to you." His heartbeat seemed to be everywhere at once. He licked his dry lips, needing to get the rest out before he lost his nerve. "I want to be with you, Sadie."

After how he'd pushed her away, he knew she deserved more than that. She deserved the absolute truth, even if his brain was screaming for him to hold in the rest before he made a complete fool of himself.

He took a couple of steps toward her, surprised his limbs were still working, since they didn't feel like they belonged to him anymore. "I love you. I've loved you since I was sixteen years old, and I'll love you until the day I die. And I just…needed you to know that."

The entire crowd took a collective breath, the rodeo grounds so still he swore even the animals didn't make a sound. Or maybe his rapid pulse thundering through his head blocked it all out.

Sadie lifted a hand to her mouth and closed her eyes. It was hard to be sure, but he thought she was crying. Just like she'd done all those years ago right before she left. He shoved the microphone toward the kid who'd brought it down to him and started away, thinking at least he'd tried. Better that than live with regrets strangling him day in and out, right?

A buzz went through the crowd, growing louder and louder, and Royce slowly turned back around.

Sadie was rushing toward the arena. She climbed the wide bars of the gate and jumped inside. He strode toward her, just short of running himself.

She met him halfway and flung herself into his arms, wrapping her legs around his waist, her hair brushing his cheek as she hugged him like she was afraid he'd float away if she didn't squeeze for all she was worth.

He wrapped his arms tightly around her, squeezing her back. "I don't want you to have to give up your dreams, but I want you to choose me this time. Even if it means figuring out how to pull off a long-distance relationship, or even if I look into moving into Nashville part-time—I'm sure we could find a way."

Sadie lifted her head and placed a hand on the side of his face, her eyes peering into his. "I love you, Royce Dixon." She pressed her mouth to his and kissed him so deeply the world around them blurred. He could hear the crowd cheering, louder applause than he'd ever gotten for winning any event. Even better, he heard it when Sadie moved her lips next to his ear and whispered, "From now on, no matter what happens, I promise I'll always choose you."

Epilogue

With CMT playing in the background, Sadie danced around the kitchen, singing and mixing her chocolate milk. She spun over to Royce's fridge and pulled out the green olives—he didn't even like them, but he always kept a jar just for her, and that always made her smile.

Most people who heard the story about her giving up a contract with Belle Meade Records looked at her like she was straitjacket crazy—except for Royce and Quinn and her family, who looked at her more like she was just slightly insane—and maybe she was.

But she was also insanely happy, and she knew they were all thrilled to have her permanently in Wyoming as well. Shortly after she'd decided to stay, she and Royce ran into Heath Brantley at the Triple S. They got to talking about how he played the guitar, and he told her he also had a friend who played the drums, and they just so happened to be looking for a singer. After booking a few gigs, gaining a decent-size fan base that spread across the entire state, and one amazing meeting where they'd been offered a contract, they'd decided to sign with an independent record company that afternoon. It'd require less travel and promo than the contract she'd almost signed—and even better, way more letting Sadie be herself.

It was perfect.

If only this damn bottle of olives would open so she could celebrate properly. She banged the edge of the lid on the counter and twisted again.

While she was running hot water over the top, seeing if that'd loosen it, she heard the front door—Royce had gone to check on the horses, but the booted steps across the floor meant he was back.

Strong arms wrapped around her waist, and then she felt his lips on her neck. "Hey, babe," he whispered against her skin. "Need some help with that?"

"No, I—" She took a deep breath and then twisted again until the muscles in her arms shook. "Got it," she finished, even though the lid refused to budge.

Royce stepped off to the side, an amused smile on his face as he watched her struggle. "Just say the word."

Sadie beat the jar on the counter again, fighting the temptation to just crack off the top—that'd show the lid. And possibly get glass in her olives, but still, results were results.

"You're gonna break it and then get mad at me for trying to help you, just like that fateful day in the grocery store. Looking back, I think that was one of the best days of my life."

"It did start something amazing," Sadie said. Then she

glared at the jar and gave it one more twist. Nothing. She looked at Royce and stuck out her lips in a pout, hoping he wouldn't actually make her ask for his help. He took the jar from her, and with a twist that made all the muscles in his forearms stand out, the lid popped loose.

"Let me guess, you got it started for me?"

"Totally." She grinned, took it from him, and tossed an olive in her mouth. Royce skimmed his hands over her hips and then pulled her flush against his warm body and kissed her. He smelled like the outdoors, hay, and sunshine, and as she soaked in every amazing detail, a happy sigh escaped her lips.

"After you called to tell me you and the guys officially signed the contract, I bought a bottle of wine. Thought we'd celebrate by opening it and watching a movie."

Royce would only take a few sips and then switch to Coors, but that was okay. Cuddling up next to him and watching a movie sounded like perfection. She nodded and tipped onto her toes to kiss him.

"Grab the corkscrew while I get the bottle and glasses?"

"Sure," she said, although she was reluctant to leave Royce's embrace. She rummaged through the utensil drawer until she found the corkscrew. When she turned around, Royce was down on a knee, something very sparkly and ringlike pinched between his fingers.

Afraid she'd accidentally faint and end up with the corkscrew embedded in her skin, she set it on the counter. Light bounced off the diamond ring as he held it up higher.

"Sadie Hart, you know I love you. I don't even want to imagine what my life would be like if you hadn't come back into it, and I promise to spend every day of the rest of it trying to make you happy. Are you ready to become my wife yet?"

She gave a laugh that was all joy and half tears. "Hell yeah!"

He slid the ring onto her finger, straightened, and drew her to him. They clung onto each other, laughing as if neither one of them could believe it. Sadie lifted her hand, studying the ring. Thick silver band with beads on the edges and lots of swirled detailing—perfectly country—with a raised square diamond in the middle. She thought of the image she'd had at the rodeo with kids in their future, and happiness filled up her heart and made more tears spill over.

Insane would've been walking away from the best thing that ever happened to her. She tilted her head up, and he leaned down, pressing his mouth to hers. Then he was parting her lips with his tongue, deepening the kiss until there was so much heat building in her body she could hardly breathe.

"Cowboy, I'm thinking the wine can wait a little while."

Royce flashed her a wicked grin that gave her even more wicked thoughts. Then he started slowly unbuttoning her shirt, his fingertips brushing her skin in that intoxicating way that drove her crazy. "This is why I'm not letting you slip through my fingers ever again. You've always got the best ideas."

Acknowledgments

This book was like coming home to me in a lot of ways. I grew up on a cattle ranch in a small town, and writing it made me miss home and all the amazing people who live there. I have to thank my dad for answering my many phone calls while I was writing this book. He talked to me about horse breeds and horse care, roping, and all the ranching terms I couldn't remember. He's why cowboys have always been heroic to me. Thanks to my uncle Keith Harmsen, for answering all the rodeo questions I had and, bonus, always being fun to talk to. Thanks to my friend Seth Vance, who came up with the name for my restaurant, and then let me use his likeness as the bartender/owner. (Although he was sure to add "be nice." As if I'd be anything but. Hehe.) And as usual, I'd never survive without Amanda Price. She's always there when I need to ask questions, vent, laugh, and everything in between. We managed to have quite the adventures growing up, and I'm glad we still manage to have some. There aren't enough words to thank her for all her support through the years.

Rachel Harris, I could write an entire paragraph about you! She's my go-to girl when I'm brainstorming, writing, and editing, and there've been many times when we suspect we share the same brain. Thanks for letting me use sexy country singer Tyler Blue in my book and for putting a Sadie cameo in yours. That was fun! Diet Mountain Dew cheers! Big hugs to Gina Maxwell, who's an awesome friend to have and someone I can happily stay up chatting with until insane hours in the morning. To the CKM, you all rock! So glad I know you!

Thanks to my editor, Stacy Abrams, for her editing prowess and for helping me through author freak-outs. My books are always better after they've been through you. Thanks to Alycia Tornetta, Debbie Suzuki, and the rest of the team at Entangled Publishing! You all are made of awesome.

My family is always so supportive and keeps me sane(ish) through the writing process. My kiddos are so excited about Mommy's books and make sure I get enough writing time, but they also force me to take breaks and remember to have fun. Michael, thank you for keeping the house running when I'm working. You've saved many dinners from being burned and many loads of laundry from that horrific mildew smell they get when I forget about them. I love you!

Shout out to Wordsmith Publicity, who is so awesome to work with and is made up of two of the coolest, funniest girls I know. Thanks to all bloggers and reviewers for helping spread the word about my book. TZWNDU, you guys are awesome and get tackle-hugs!

And last but not least, thank you to my readers. I heart you all!

About the Author

Cindi Madsen sits at her computer every chance she gets, plotting, revising, and falling in love with her characters. Sometimes it makes her a crazy person. Without it, she'd be even crazier. She has way too many shoes but can always find a reason to buy a new pretty pair, especially if they're sparkly, colorful, or super-tall. She loves music, dancing, and wishes summer lasted all year long. She lives in Colorado (where summer is most definitely NOT all year long) with her husband and three children. She is the author of YA books *All the Broken Pieces*, *Cipher*, and *Demons of the Sun* and adult romances *Falling for Her Fiancé*, *Act Like You Love Me*, *Resisting the Hero*, *An Officer and a Rebel*, *Cinderella Screwed Me Over*, and *Ready to Wed*. You can visit Cindi at: www.cindimadsen.com, where you can sign up for her newsletter to get all the up-to-date information on her books. Follow her on Twitter @cindimadsen.

Also by Cindi Madsen

RESISTING THE HERO

FALLING FOR HER FIANCE

ACT LIKE YOU LOVE ME

AN OFFICER AND A REBEL

Be wooed by Cindi Madsen's single title romances...

READY TO WED

CINDERELLA SCREWED ME OVER

ALL THE BROKEN PIECES

Made in the USA
Monee, IL
27 November 2022

18643396R00125